The Veins of the South Are Still Open

AF512258

The Veins of the South Are Still Open

Debates Around the Imperialism of Our Time

Edited, with an Introduction, by
Emiliano López

LeftWord

First published in September 2020

LeftWord Books
2254/2A Shadi Khampur
New Ranjit Nagar
New Delhi 110008
INDIA

LeftWord Books is the publishing division of
Naya Rasta Publishers Pvt. Ltd.

Individual essays © respective authors, 2020
This collection © LeftWord Books, 2020

leftword.com

ISBN 978-81-945925-1-8 (PB)
978-81-945925-7-0 (Ebook)

CONTENTS

EMILIANO LÓPEZ

A TOOLBOX TO CLOSE OUR VEINS

> In these lands we are not experiencing the primitive infancy of capitalism, but its vicious senility.
>
> Eduardo Galeano, *Open Veins of Latin America*

> Fence spent the night there: at dawn it crawled toward the canyon where the highway hurries off to Huánuco. Two uncrossable mountains guard the pass: reddish Pucamina and Yantacaca, always in mourning; even the birds can't fly over them. . . . On the fifth day the Fence outdid the birds.
>
> Manuel Scorza, *Redoble por Rancas*

The concept of imperialism has a bad reputation. Without any doubt, within the intellectual and hegemonic academic world it is treated as a *démodé* term, mainly ideologic and with low explanatory capacity for our current reality. But in this 'Era of Globalization', we do not need to re-edit categories from other historical moments that would lead us to repeat old formulae to improve the life of our people. We need to know the time we are living in and give priority to realism. Even though it may be motivated by noble intentions, this vision paralyses us at the same time as it convinces us about the fact that an unequal world can just be transformed in its molecular dimension. However, it is part of the triumph of the Western and capitalist civilizing model after the fall of the Berlin Wall that a good part of critical thinking has abandoned certain categories in pursuit of explanations which are more friendly to the academic and political establishment of our time. Whichever way we look at it, in the Global South we find situations that require global explanations.

The appropriation of common goods in Africa and Latin America; the expansion of textile workshops in inhuman working conditions in Asia; the control of production of the countries from Southern Europe and Northern Africa by companies based in Germany and France; the domination of the State of Israel over Palestine; the imposition of private property over communal spaces, transforming them into spaces for capital accumulation; the countless military interventions in the Middle East; the imposition of the 'American way of life' through the American cultural industry—all these are just some of the expressions of the fact that global capitalism is, as Samir Amin put it, an 'unequal system between countries and regions'. Inequality is not an abstraction or a mere theoretical speculation; it makes itself tangible in the bodies of the oppressed from the South.

This is why we consider that imperialism is the most appropriate category to understand this global inequality. We think it is urgent to give substance, according to our current times and struggles, to a powerful concept in explicative and historical terms associated with the struggles of peoples for their liberation. Imperialism is both a concept and a native category of our emancipation projects from the South. The history of this theoretical and political concept is widely spread.

Towards the end of the nineteenth century, Great Britain met its strongest capitalist expansionary period. After suffering a heavy economic crisis, a new impulse of its own capitalism implied a new wave of global expansion of the Western capitalist civilization. Here, the most significant novelty in relation to the previous colonial practices was that the expansion in response, mainly, to the needs of capital accumulation in the industrial centres of Europe. As it has been noted by J.A. Hobson, a liberal critic of the imposition of English government on the rest of the world,

> It is admitted by all business men that the growth of the powers of production in their countries exceeds the growth in consumption, that more goods can be produced than can be sold at a profit, and that more capital exists than can find remunerative investment. ... It is this economic condition of affairs that forms the taproot of Imperialism.

This interpretation motivated Marxist thinkers as Lenin, Rosa Luxemburg, and Kautsky to look at this new stage that would open in the world. Lenin's work *Imperialism, the Highest Stage of Capitalism* marked a before and an after in the debate about imperialism. This concept not only explained the concentration of power and the incomes of the Northern countries, but it was also a mechanism for capital concentration and monopolization, based in the exportation of capital from the imperialist countries towards the world's peripheries and favoured by the development of financial capital and the simultaneous appropriation of the resources that came from the South to guarantee Northern productive conditions.

To a large extent, we can see these years of global expansion of Northern capital, the English one in particular, as a jumble of capitalism and colonialism. In fact, much of the operation of this apparently civilizing process of the North was based in the economic liberalization and political dependency of a quarter of the world. Asia, Africa and the Middle East were divided as property of different imperialist countries of Europe. Hence, a quarter of the world was distributed into colonies which imposed with bloodshed and fire the new 'ought to be' of transnational corporations.

In the case of Latin America, imperialism adopted the shape of economic dependency in a frame of presumed national policy independence. As presented by Manuel Scorza in his magnificent and heartbreaking story, foreign capital got installed in our lands, appropriating water, hills and life itself. Apart from this expansion, global capital entered a new and terrible phase of crisis. A war without precedent until now, which destroyed the centres of classic imperialism, was the most dehumanizing expression of this new phase of development of the unequal world order. It is in this context that a new global hegemony emerged which was consolidated after the Second World War: United States. Far from trying to fan the conflict between powers, the United States became the best representative of American capital and global capital for, at least, fifty years. It encouraged the reconstruction of Europe to obtain profitable markets for its domestic industrial expansion, it made negotiations possible to promote flows of productive investments in Southern countries, it exported its cultural consumption patterns around the world, it openly participated in the military operations against the left projects of several countries and imposed military regimes in a variety of Southern countries.

As the historian Perry Anderson has correctly said, the United States based its new imperial logic in a combination of the productive strength of its economy, its capacity for military domination and its hegemonic capacity through the legitimacy of its democracy and cultural model. It is, to a great extent, 'an iron fist inside a velvet glove'. Beyond the triumph of the American imperialism, the popular resistances in the Global South during the '60s, the Cuban Revolution, and the defeat of the empire in Vietnam marked a new political crisis in this unequal order while it developed a new global economic crisis—maybe the most significant one—to explain the world we are living in today. The crisis in the '70s found, again, its way out in reloaded imperialism. Neoliberalism and imperialism twinned to give place to a new cycle of financial, productive and military impositions from the North to the South. The new global (dis)order that was born during the capitalist crisis in the '70s multiplied the previous inequalities and generated a tendency towards financialization and an unprecedented plundering. After declaring the 'death of ideology' and the 'end of history' in favour of a new, free, democratic and capitalist global world, the potential new American century is, again, in an undeniable crisis.

But this crisis does not have any conditions of more dignity for the people of the South. On the contrary, the American imperialist crisis highlights barbarism: direct military intervention in the Middle East, multiplication of its financial impositions, absorption of the world's capital masses turning them into financial capital, development of new formats of hybrid wars against countries that do not want to give up sovereignty, from Syria to Venezuela. This book tries to build a new interpretation of imperialism in our time from a conversational and collective debate. It is a toolbox to understand our time and renew our commitment against any form of oppression.

Understanding how imperialism acts today, through which mechanism it acts, defining the depth of its crisis and the possibilities of alternative hegemonies allow us to re-edit our commitment to the liberation of our people in the Global South. It helps us realize that, to the greatest extent possible, we should close the wound that implies the spoliation of our bodies, our culture, our common goods and our jobs. It allows us to reconstruct a historical base on which we can stand, what Che Guevara synthesized, in that beyond the tactical disagreements, 'as for the great strategic objective—the total destruction of imperialism by means of struggle—on that we must be intransigent'.

We include here five chapters that go through a variety of points of debate against the interpretations that celebrate neoliberal globalization, against the 'there's no choice' argument. They call into question the role that imperialist countries give to our Southern economies as the ones that guarantee cheap food; the new (old) forms of labour exploitation; the characteristics of competence between large-scale capitals; a new military strategy of the United States in the context of the crisis of its hegemonic project; and the nodal points to interpret the hegemonic succession we are living in as an opportunity and as a risk at the same time.

We expect these to be a contribution to understanding the monstrosity of our enemy, but at the same time to lead us to sharpen our tools and strengthen our trenches. Because, ultimately, as terrible as the enemy's actions are, we will always fight for our dreams of justice. As the Palestinian poet Samih Al-Qassem said in his 'Address from the Unemployment Bureau',

> By night a torch might be extinguished.
> I might be denied my mother's kiss.
> My people—father, son, daughter—
>   might be cursed.
> A coward might just forge my history,
>   an idolized superstitious man.
> You might sneak up on my sorrow's guard
> while it's napping, deprive my children of holiday suits,
> deceive my friends with a face that's false;
> you can raise a wall around me,
>   and around me,
>   and around me,
> or crucify my days on disgrace! But O Enemy of the Sun!
> I will resist
>   to the final pulse in my veins!

UTSA PATNAIK AND PRABHAT PATNAIK

IMPERIALISM IN THE ERA OF GLOBALIZATION[1]

INTRODUCTION

Capitalism is pre-eminently a money-using system where a large part of wealth is held either in the form of money, or as money-denominated assets, namely financial assets. It is essential for the system to work that the value of money should not keep declining against commodities; otherwise people would move away from holding money, and it would cease to be not just a form of wealth, but even a medium of circulation.

Capitalism ensures the stability of the value of money in a number of ways. One is the maintenance of a vast reserve army of labour, not just within the metropolis but also in the Third World. This 'distant' reserve army too keeps down not only local money wages and hence the prices of raw materials produced there, but also the money wages of workers in the metropolis, who are threatened with unemployment through capital outflows to the Third World, in the event of their insisting on higher wages.

These reserve armies, however, are not enough. Even if there is no autonomous increase in raw material prices and money wages

[1] This article was authorized to be included in this book by the editors of *Monthly Review*. We thank the authors and editors of the journal for the possibility of including this valuable article in our publication. For the original version of the text, see Utsa Patnaik and Prabhat Patnaik, 'Imperialism in the Era of Globalization', *Monthly Review*, vol. 67, no. 3 (July–August 2015).—*Ed.*

because of their existence, certain scarce commodities would still experience a price rise as capital accumulation increases the demand for them. The threat this poses to the value of money has also to be warded off, and this is done by restricting the demand for such commodities outside the capitalist sector, through a squeeze on mass purchasing power there (i.e. by imposing an 'income deflation'). Two typical instruments of such 'income deflation' historically have been the siphoning off without any *quid pro quo* of the surplus produced there (Indian anti-colonial economists had called this the 'drain of wealth'), and the destruction of petty production there through imports from the capitalist metropolis (what the same writers had called 'deindustrialization'), which had created the 'distant' reserve army in the first place. This entire arrangement, encompassing the world outside of capitalism proper, constitutes 'imperialism'. It does not end with colonialism; on the contrary its importance increases with 'financialization' when stability of the value of money becomes a matter of even greater overriding concern (whence the current obsession with 'inflation targeting').

Imperialism as an arrangement, however, has remained largely invisible to the discipline of economics, even to its best practitioners and even in the colonial period. No less a person than John Maynard Keynes, in his classic work *The Economic Consequences of the Peace* (1919), where he talks of the 'economic *Eldorado*' that prewar Europe represented, fails to mention that this *Eldorado* rested upon an elaborate framework of imperialism. Europe's accessing of food from the 'new world', an important aspect of this *Eldorado*, would not have been possible if this food had not been paid for, through an intricate arrangement, by Britain's appropriation *gratis* of a part of the surplus of its colonies and semi-colonies ('drain of wealth'), and by its export of manufactured goods to its colonies and semi-colonies at the expense of their local producers ('de-industrialization'[2]).

Imperialism, however, is not just some phenomenon limited to history. It necessarily underlies, as already mentioned, capitalism in all its epochs including the current era of globalization. Let us examine the issue in detail.

I

Economists have always been haunted by the spectre of 'diminishing returns'. Ricardo had famously seen 'diminishing returns' in agriculture leading to a progressive fall in the rate of profit, a progressive shift of the terms of trade between manufacturing and agriculture in favour of the latter and the eventual *denouement* of a stationary state where further growth became impossible. Even Keynes in the aforementioned work saw 'diminishing returns' in food production as undermining the *Eldorado* even if the war had not done so. And yet none of these fears have come true. The terms of trade between manufacturing and agriculture have shown a secular tendency to shift *against*, rather than *in favour of*, the latter;[3] and while the growth rate under capitalism has come down of late, this has nothing to do with any fall in the profit rate caused by 'diminishing returns'. Likewise, the

2 For the role of such 'drain' of surplus and 'deindustrialization' see A.K. Bagchi, *Perilous Passage: The Global Ascendancy of Capital*, Delhi: Oxford University Press, 2006; and Utsa Patnaik, 'The Free Lunch: Transfers from the Tropical Colonies and their Role in Capital Formation in Britain During the Industrial Revolution', in *Globalization Under Hegemony: The Long Twentieth Century*, ed. K.S. Jomo, Delhi: Oxford University Press, 2006, pp. 30–70.

3 For a recent estimate of the secular movement in the terms of trade, see Shouvik Chakraborty, 'Movements in the Terms of Trade of Primary Commodities vis-à-vis manufactured Goods: A Theoretical and Empirical Study', Ph.D. thesis, Centre for Economic Studies and Planning, Jawaharlal Nehru University, New Delhi, 2011.

advanced capitalist world has no difficulty to this day in meeting its food requirements, belying the fears of Keynes. How then do we explain this contrast between fears and reality?

We cannot simply claim that 'diminishing returns' are a myth. The limitation of land-size is without doubt a material reality to reckon with. Land-size of course can be augmented, not in natural but in effective units, through yield-raising technological progress, or through certain kinds of investment such as irrigation which make multiple cropping possible. In other words, 'land-augmenting' measures are certainly possible. But in their absence, the limitations of land-size would raise over time, as demand increases, the 'real cost' of agricultural output (to use Keynes's term), which means that, for a given money wage and money prices of other inputs, the supply price of this output will increase over time as more of it is produced.

Such an increase in supply price, however, creates serious problems for capitalism. These arise not because of a diminishing rate of profit or a slide towards a stationary state as Ricardo had feared. Such fears relate in any case to *long-run* prospects. Increasing supply price, in so far as it gets translated to an increase in price, undermines the value of money, and that is a very serious and *immediate* issue for capitalism. If wealth-holders believe that the value of money in terms of commodities is going to fall over time, then nobody will hold wealth in its money-form.

It may be thought that since all other commodities have positive carrying costs while money has none, a shift from money to some commodity as the form of holding wealth will take place only if some minimum rate of inflation in the price of that commodity is expected to occur (for which it must first occur and therefore be expected) which outweighs its carrying cost; and if this threshold inflation rate is not reached then no shift from money to this commodity will occur at all.

But two points must be noted here. One, if *some* people

expect the rate of inflation to exceed the rate of carrying cost on a commodity, even while the majority do not, then they would shift from money to that commodity; this, however, would force the price of that commodity upwards, and make *some more people* also shift from money to that commodity because of revised expectations regarding its price, and so on. And if because of increasing supply price, nobody expects that commodity's price to *fall*, then an inflationary process so begun will eliminate money from its role of a wealth-form.

Secondly, and more importantly, within agricultural lands, the *tropical* land-mass occupies a special position. Its size is *absolutely* fixed (in the absence of 'land-augmenting' measures) but it produces a range of products for capitalism that are simply not producible elsewhere though of vital importance for it. Indeed the raw material central to the original industrial revolution that got capitalism going—raw cotton—was not producible in the metropolis, but could only be produced in the tropical and sub-tropical regions. Hence, as accumulation proceeds in the metropolis, the supply price for a range of products producible on the *fixed* tropical land-mass would shoot up. The consequent inflation rate would far exceed any threshold rate for shifting from money to commodities.

Any such increasing supply price therefore is fundamentally incompatible with the role of money as a form of wealth-holding. And since even holding money for transaction purposes entails a holding of wealth in money-form, no matter for how fleeting a moment, anything that eliminates money as a wealth-form *ipso facto* also eliminates money as a medium of circulation, and hence makes a monetary economy impossible. Such increasing supply price therefore is fundamentally incompatible with a monetary economy.

It is essential for the viability of the capitalist system that this phenomenon of increasing supply price must not be allowed to manifest itself. And this is exactly what has happened throughout the history of capitalism, which is why the Ricardian prognostications or even the Keynesian anticipations have *never actually materialized*. They have not materialized not because diminishing returns are a myth, but because capitalism has taken recourse to other ways of ensuring that they do not materialize.

Imperialism is one such device, which ensures that the phenomenon of increasing supply price does not actually manifest itself. In fact, as we shall see, it is not just one *possible* device, but *the* device typically used by capitalism for this purpose, whence it follows that imperialism is immanent in the money-form itself. Let us see why and how imperialism becomes germane to this entire issue.

II

Let us discuss agriculture first before coming to extractive industries whose case is similar. The fixed size of the tropical landmass would not be a problem if land-augmenting investment or land-augmenting technical progress could take place to a degree sufficient to offset increasing supply price. But these typically require public investment. Irrigation in the tropical regions for multiple cropping, as Marx had noted long ago,[4] requires the State, since the scale of investment far exceeds what is possible or even profitable for an individual producer, who typically happens to be a petty producer. Even land-augmenting technical progress in the form of newer practices requires research which only the State can undertake and disseminate widely for reducing risks for the petty producers. (Even when multinational corporations develop and disseminate new varieties of seeds and other inputs that can raise

[4] Karl Marx, 'The British Rule in India', *The New York Daily Tribune*, June 25, 1853; reprinted in *Marx on India*, ed. Iqbal Husain, New Delhi: Tulika Books, 2006.

yields, the degree to which these innovations get adopted depends upon the availability of subsidized credit and other inputs which the State provides.)

But where the State is constrained to follow the principle of 'sound finance'—as was the case in tropical countries prior to decolonization, when the State tried to balance its budget, and as is the case again under globalization when 'fiscal responsibility', in the sense of a 3 per cent or less fiscal deficit–GDP ratio, has become the 'norm'—such initiatives from the State become conspicuous by their absence. The *spontaneous* tendency under capitalism (i.e. excepting its transitory post-colonial *dirigiste* phase) is to eschew 'land augmentation'.

Preventing increasing supply price from manifesting itself therefore typically takes the form of suppressing the *ex post* demand for such commodities even as their *ex ante* demand increases. The non-increase in *ex post* demand in effect means that the phenomenon of increasing supply price does not manifest itself.

The suppression of *ex post* demand can itself be done in two ways: one is through what Keynes had called 'profit inflation', i.e. a *rise* in prices relative to *given* money wage-bills and money income-bills of the working people; the other is through what one may call 'income deflation', i.e. a *fall* in money wage-bills and money income-bills of the working people for given prices. The first of these entails once more a threat to the value of money and hence to the stability of the monetary system.

True, one can imagine a situation where profit inflation is *localized*, posing no threat to the metropolitan currencies, i.e. where the rise in prices relative to money wages occurs in a particular non-metropolitan country or set of countries, whose exchange rate depreciates correspondingly vis-à-vis the metropolitan currencies. But even such localization of profit inflation would necessarily undermine the value of the local money and thereby destroy the local monetary system; and what is more, a flight from money to commodities *within* that set of countries could raise some commodity prices even in terms of metropolitan currencies, and hence cause problems for the value of money in the metropolis. Hence, even though such profit inflation does occur, the more favoured means of suppressing *ex post* demand under capitalism, to prevent the manifestation of increasing supply price, is income deflation. A whole range of instruments are used to ensure that *ex post* demand for commodities with increasing supply price is suppressed, through a squeeze on the money incomes of the working people.[5]

The question arises: working people where? The preservation of the value of money in the metropolis by preventing any manifestation of increasing supply price can be ensured through imposing income deflation *upon any segment of the working population that demands the particular commodity*. In other words, income deflation may be imposed on the working people either in the metropolis or in the periphery (or both); in either case it would serve its purpose. But it seems unrealistic to imagine that the working people in the periphery would be spared while those in the metropolis would be squeezed. If anything, the social stability of metropolitan capitalism would require the very opposite of this, namely to shift the burden of income deflation as much as possible to the periphery. Hence the conclusion emerges: metropolitan capitalism *necessarily imposes income deflation upon the working people of the periphery, including even upon the very petty producers whose products are subject to increasing supply price ex ante (i.e. at unchanged rates of money earnings for them).*

The fact that metropolitan capitalism necessarily imposes income deflation upon the working people of the periphery

5 For a discussion in the Indian context see Utsa Patnaik, 'Deflationary Neo-liberalism: An Indian Perspective', in *National Perspectives on Globalization: A Critical Reader*, eds. P. Bowles, H. Veltmeyer et al., London: Palgrave, 2007.

remains unaltered no matter what phase of capitalism we talk about, and no matter what else happens in that phase. *It is a defining characteristic of imperialism.* In an exclusively capitalist world where even the 'diminishing returns' activities are within the capitalist sector, such as the situation Ricardo had visualized, the term 'imperialism' will have no meaning; wage deflation within capitalism will then be the sole form of income deflation. But when there are other modes of production and classes which have a spatially distinct existence (such as in the tropical land-mass or the periphery in general, as distinct from metropolitan capitalism which is primarily located in the temperate regions), then the imposition of income deflation has a spatial dimension too; and this spatiality has been traditionally referred to and captured by the term imperialism.

In the current period when the weight of finance has increased, the urgency to preserve the value of money has become even greater. Hence the need to impose income deflation generally, and upon the working people of the periphery in particular, has become even more pressing. Imperialism, far from disappearing, has become even more significant. That a segment of the periphery's bourgeoisie has become integrated with metropolitan capital, that some countries in the periphery have experienced high 'growth', that the working people in the metropolis are now experiencing income deflation to a far greater extent than before, are all differences to be registered regarding the contemporary capitalist world in contrast with its past. But having registered them, we must also make clear that they make not an iota of difference to the reality of imperialism, i.e. to the fact of the imposition of income deflation by metropolitan capital on the working people of the periphery.

It may seem to some that this reality of imperialism is only in focus when we are looking at the limited sphere of agriculture as we have been doing so far. Quite apart from the fact that in the global picture that sphere is far from limited, all that has been said so far about agriculture, especially the products of the tropical land-mass, holds equally for extractive industries. The imposition of income deflation upon the working people of the periphery is also a means of ensuring that the problem of increasing supply price does not manifest itself with regard to the products of extractive industries.

Extractive industries, however, have an additional specificity, namely that unlike a land-mass cultivated by vast numbers of peasants, minerals are to be found in specific locations whose ownership can be easily monopolized. Metropolitan capital therefore always tries to monopolize this ownership. In a period of inter-imperialist rivalry, there is rivalry among the different segments of metropolitan capital to acquire ownership, not just of actual mineral sources but even of potential ones, as Lenin had argued. But in periods like the present, globalization, leading to the formation of an *international* finance capital (as distinct from a mere international agreement between national finance capitals, such as Karl Kautsky had visualized), mutes inter-imperialist rivalries generally, including rivalry for ownership and control over actual and potential sources of mineral wealth. Its being brought under the neoliberal regime, as opposed to being under the control of the periphery's State, is what is generally insisted upon by all shades of metropolitan capital.

III

The old imperialism, i.e. imperialism *with* colonies, used the colonial State to impose income deflation upon the working people of the periphery, so that their absorption of what the periphery itself produced could be curtailed and the commodities so released could either be directly taken to the metropolis, or could make way for the production of other commodities demanded by the metropolis, towards which the land hitherto used for their production could shift. The two main forms of income deflation were: the colonial taxation system, with a large part of the revenue being used to buy these commodities which thus accrued *gratis* to the colonial power as the 'drain of surplus' mentioned earlier; and the creation of unemployment through the destruction of local crafts by imports from the metropolis, i.e. the process of 'deindustrialization' mentioned earlier. 'Deindustrialization' also directly released commodities hitherto locally absorbed, such as raw materials used up in textile production and foodgrains that had gone into the subsistence of the now displaced petty producers.

The old imperialism had the 'advantage' that the leading metropolitan power of the time, Britain, could keep its economy open to the goods of the then newly-industrializing countries, *without getting indebted* (on the contrary it became the largest capital exporter in the years before the First World War). For at least four decades up to 1928, India had the second largest export surplus in the world (second only to the USA); and this despite the imports of goods that caused domestic de-industrialization. But this export surplus was entirely appropriated by Britain not only to pay for its current account deficit with continental Europe, North America and regions of recent European settlement, but also to allow it to export capital to these regions.[6] This contrasts with the position of the leading metropolitan power of today, the United States, which is also the most highly indebted country in the world, with a rapidly growing debt. The difference between the two situations arises because colonial markets and colonial 'drain' can no longer play the same role as before, though no doubt the phenomena of market encroachment and drain of surplus continue, the latter in the form *inter alia* of superprofits from technological

6 See Utsa Patnaik, 'India in the World Economy 1900 to 1935: The Inter-War Depression and Britain's Demise as World Capitalist Leader', *Social Scientist*, vol. 42, nos. 1–2 (January–February 2014).

monopoly, now institutionalized by the TRIPS (Agreement on Trade-Related Aspects of Intellectual Property Rights) agreement.

The reduced importance of the drain of surplus and of the markets of the periphery arises not just because of political decolonization, but also because the scope for further encroaching on these markets which have already been penetrated is limited, while the current needs of metropolitan capitalism are enormous.

In contemporary capitalism, in contrast to the colonial period, the enforcement of neoliberal policies is the chief means of imposing income deflation on the working people of the periphery. There are at least five obvious ways in which these policies bring about income deflation for the working people in the periphery. The most obvious is through a massive increase in income inequalities. The large labour reserves which exist in the periphery in countries like India, China, Indonesia, and Bangladesh, far from getting used up, actually increase in relative size, which keeps down the real wages not only of the working people in the periphery, but also of the workers in the metropolis. This is because the workers in the metropolis now have to compete with those in the periphery, because of the willingness of metropolitan capital, a willingness that did not exist earlier, to move to locations in the periphery for setting up production units for meeting not local but metropolitan needs. The vector of world real wages therefore does not show any increase; it even decreases.[7] But labour productivity increases everywhere, resulting in a rise in the share of surplus. This imposes income deflation on the working people, even while, at the same time, creating a tendency towards global 'over-production'.

The second way in which income deflation is imposed on them under neoliberalism is through the government's fiscal measures.

[7] For the United States for instance, Joseph Stiglitz says: 'Adjusted for inflation, real wages have stagnated or fallen; a typical male worker's income in 2011 ($32,986) was lower than it was in 1968 ($33,880).' *New York Times*, January 13, 2013.

Given the fact that economies get opened to global capital flows, including global financial flows, governments vie with one another to offer fiscal concessions to globalized capital to entice it to locate plants on their soils for bringing about 'development'. At the same time, since 'fiscal responsibility' enjoins a limit on the relative size of the fiscal deficit, tax concessions to capital are necessarily matched by cuts in social expenditures, in transfers to the poor, in food subsidies, and in public provisioning of essential services like health and education, all of which hurt the working people, and all of which reduce in real terms the purchasing power in their hands. The income deflation so effected restricts their consumption of essential goods like foodgrains, so that the use of the limited landmass for meeting the demands of the rich becomes possible without posing any threat to the value of money; what accompanies this process, however, is growing hunger among people.

The following figures illustrate the point. Taking the world as a whole, between the triennium 1979–81 and the triennium 1999–2001, per capita cereal output (average annual output divided by population of the middle year) fell from 355 kilograms to 343 kilograms. (Calculations for the triennium 2015–17 also put the figure at 345 kilograms.[8]) With the world per capita income rising, since the income elasticity of demand for cereals is positive and since no major stock de-cumulation took place in 1999–2001 compared to 1979–81, one would have expected a significant increase in cereal prices over these two decades, and hence also a shift in the terms of trade in favour of cereals vis-à-vis manufacturing. In fact, however, these terms of trade *declined for cereals* by 46 per cent between 1979–81 and 1999–2001![9] The virulence of the income deflation imposed upon the working people, especially in the periphery, may be gauged from this.

The third way is through a reduction in the share of the

[8] The cereal output data are taken from the Food and Agriculture Organization.

[9] We are grateful to Dr. Shouvik Chakraborty for giving us this figure.

petty producers in the aggregate value added in the entire chain from the harvest to the retail market. This occurs because petty traders with little bargaining strength, and government marketing agencies that earlier existed to give a 'fair' share to producers are increasingly replaced by monopoly capitalists, including multinational corporations.

The fourth way is through a continuation of the colonial process of displacement of local petty producers and local petty traders by big business including multinational corporations. The phenomenon of 'deindustrialization' now spreads to the tertiary sector as well, where Walmart and other such corporations precipitate a new round of displacement-cum-unemployment. Such a fate also awaits craftsmen, fishermen and a host of petty producers.

The fifth and the last way is in many ways the most significant, namely the unleashing of a process of primitive accumulation of capital vis-à-vis the peasantry, where large capital, in the name of 'development', and 'infrastructure', takes over not just common land or government land but even land of the peasants at 'throwaway' prices. The imposition of income deflation on the peasantry affects not just the demand side but also the supply side of agricultural commodities; this only means, however, that for the preservation of the value of money, the squeeze on demand has to be even greater.

'Globalization' thus greatly accelerates the process of separation of petty producers from their means of production. At the same time, it also adds to the size of the global reserve army of labour, and helps to ensure that it does not get depleted.[10]

IV

The existence of a pool of unemployed and underemployed

[10] The discussion which follows has benefited greatly from John Bellamy Foster, R.W. McChesney, and R.J. Jonna's paper 'The Global Reserve Army of Labor and the New Imperialism', *Monthly Review*, vol. 63, no. 6 (November 2011).

labour itself acts as a measure of income deflation; but it also prevents any possibility of a money wage-push, a prevention that is vital for the preservation of the value of money.[11]

The usual discussion of the role of the reserve army in the Marxist tradition has tended to emphasize the restraint it places on *real wages*, and hence the fact that it keeps the process of exploitation going. This is the way that Marx himself discussed the subject. But while, in Marx's theory, changes in money and real wages went together, as he was focusing on a universe with 'commodity-money', in a world with credit money these two changes need not go together. It is not enough in such a world that there should be a restraining factor, from the point of view of capital, upon the level of *real wages*; there should also be a restraining factor upon the level of *money wages*.

The reserve army in such a world therefore plays the role of stabilizing the monetary system by keeping down the level of money wages. It does not just preserve the process of appropriation of surplus-value; it also keeps the monetary system going, for which of course the size of the reserve army has to be large enough. In the era of globalization, when the international mobility of capital links the wages of workers in the metropolis with those of the workers in the periphery, the reserve army itself plays a global role. *Even if not located in the metropolis itself, it plays a global role, of keeping down the vector of money wages across all countries, including the metropolis, and imparting stability to the metropolitan monetary system.* The maintenance of a global reserve army thus complements the process of income deflation and is an integral part of the operation of imperialism.

The global reserve army is in general spontaneously reproduced, and even increased in relative size, in the era of globalization. The increasing global income inequalities raise *ceteris paribus* the

11 The discussion which follows is based on P. Patnaik, *The Value of Money*, New York: Columbia University Press, 2009.

rate of growth of labour productivity. This is because the rich on average not only demand less employment-intensive products than the poor but also move to newer and newer products more rapidly, which typically are less and less employment-intensive. For any given rate of output growth, therefore, the rate of growth of employment slows down under globalization.

True, the rate of output growth itself has been higher in some peripheral economies in the era of globalization, but even this has not been enough to prevent a relative increase in the labour reserves, as the term 'jobless growth' used in the context of economies like India suggests.[12] *An even more important source for replenishing and enlarging the reserve army is, as we have seen, the process of primitive accumulation of capital which gets intensified in the era of globalization and throws vast numbers of displaced petty producers on a job market where the rise in demand for labour is just not rapid enough.*

An implication of the foregoing should be noted. The non-depletion of the reserve army of labour in peripheral economies is important not just for the bourgeoisies of these economies, but for metropolitan capital as well. It follows that the belief that with growth in peripheral economies, a state of labour shortage will arise there sooner or later, putting an upward pressure on wages and hence eliminating poverty, is a naïve one: any such *denouement* will be associated with a collapse of the monetary system in the metropolis, which the latter will fiercely resist, along with the local big bourgeoisie that is now integrated with it.

[12] Between 2004–05 and 2009–10 for instance when the India's GDP was apparently growing at over 7 per cent per annum, the number of those whose 'usual status' is being employed increased at an annual rate of 0.8 percent, according to the National Sample Survey, which is much lower than the rate of growth of labour supply.

V

Imperialism subserves a whole range of requirements of capitalism, such as acquiring external markets and ensuring the supply of raw materials, without which, as Harry Magdoff had pointed out,[13] there would be no manufacturing whatsoever, no matter how small its share in the gross value of manufacturing output. All these requirements persist in the era of globalization, but one in particular comes to the forefront, precisely because of the overarching presence of finance, and that concerns the preservation of the value of money. A set of processes associated with capitalism in the era of globalization which are not confined to the metropolis but affect the periphery deeply, spontaneously work towards this end. The intensified process of primitive accumulation of capital (which as Rosa Luxemburg had pointed out is not confined only to the pre-history of capitalism but accompanies it throughout its history); the replenishing and enlarging of labour reserves in the periphery because of such primitive accumulation and also because of the high rates of labour productivity growth *within the capitalist segment*; the pursuit of neoliberal policies which unleash a process of income deflation quite apart from what ensues because of the increase in the relative size of the global reserve army—are all part of this phenomenon. All these processes which enmesh the periphery in their web constitute key elements of contemporary imperialism. All of them constitute impositions upon the working people in the periphery against which they are powerless to act, notwithstanding political decolonization, unless they de-link their economies from a regime of liberalized capital and trade flows.

It is often argued that during the '50s, '60s and the '70s, when the leading capitalist power, the United States, actually engineered

[13] Harry Magdoff, *The Age of Imperialism*, New York: Monthly Review Press, 1969.

the overthrow of governments from Mossadegh to Árbenz to Allende that were attempting to acquire greater control over their national resources at the expense of multinational corporations, imperialism was a real phenomenon; but not so now. In other words, while imperialism was a meaningful term earlier, not just in the colonial era but even in the postwar decades, it is no longer so now.

Our argument is precisely the opposite of this. Imperialism became *visible* because the *dirigiste regimes* that came up in former colonies after decolonization, sought in various ways to overthrow its yoke. They sought to acquire greater control over national resources; they jettisoned the principle of 'sound finance' even as they raised taxes on domestic and foreign capitalists, using the public sector as a fallback option in the event of capitalist resistance and non-cooperation; they carried out 'land-augmenting' investment and technical progress under the aegis of the public sector which obviated the need for any income deflation; and they committed the State to the task of provisioning essential services. All this meant a loosening of the imperial stranglehold, which is why imperialism was so *visible* in opposing these regimes.

But with the imposition of neoliberal policies in the era of globalization, the scope for any independent action on the part of the nation-State against globalized finance, which can leave its shores when it pleases, gets greatly curtailed. Put differently, the Third World State undergoes a change from the *dirigiste* era to the neoliberal era: from being a State (even if a bourgeois State) that apparently stands above all classes intervening for the 'social good', and hence on occasion even on behalf of the oppressed, to one that promotes almost exclusively the interests of the corporate-financial oligarchy, which is integrated with globalized capital, on the grounds that its interests are coterminous with 'social interest'. With this change in the nature of the State, from a *dirigiste* to a neoliberal State, that is effected everywhere through the process of globalization, the need for any explicit imperialist intervention disappears (except for acquiring direct control over oil, as in Iraq). *In short, the invisibility of imperialism today means that it has become far more powerful, not that it has disappeared.*

VI

There is more to this power of imperialism than the mere possibility of capital flight. Globalization tends systematically to undermine all possibilities of resistance in the periphery against the hegemony of international finance capital. The growth in the relative size of the reserve army makes trade-union action difficult; and labour rights are undermined in the name of introducing 'labour market flexibility' for attracting capital to boost 'development'. It also gives rise to privatization of public sector units, 'outsourcing' of work to the unorganized sector, the substitution of casual labour for full-time workers, a shift towards 'domestic production' at extraordinarily low wages, all of which make organized workers' resistance difficult. Simultaneously, the dispossession of the peasantry, the income deflation imposed upon it, also tends to make peasant action that much more difficult. The two 'basic classes' therefore get weakened.

But this only means that *traditional forms of class resistance* become more difficult to replicate, and new forms of resistance must be developed. To distract from the economic hardships they bring to the people under globalization, neoliberal regimes seek to find political props for their survival by promoting ethnic, religious and other forms of sectarian strife in society. In doing so, they contribute towards a disintegration of social life. Such a tendency, however, also creates the conditions for an overthrow of neoliberalism, and a movement through stages towards a transcendence of capitalism, as it increasingly makes clear to the people that the choice, as Rosa Luxemburg had put it, is between socialism and barbarism.

JOHN SMITH

EXPLOITATION AND SUPER-EXPLOITATION IN THE THEORY OF IMPERIALISM

IMPERIALISM AND ITS DENIERS

'Communism is not a doctrine but a *movement*; it proceeds not from principles but from *facts*' (Engels [1847] 2010, p. 303). Wide international differences in the rate of exploitation, the huge global shift of production and of the centre of gravity of the industrial working class to countries and regions where exploitation is most intense, the dramatically heightened dependency of firms headquartered in imperialist countries (and likewise of prosperity and social peace in those countries) on the proceeds of this exploitation—these are the most important facts about the so-called neoliberal capitalism from which we must proceed.

Extreme rates of exploitation in Bangladeshi garment factories, Chinese production lines, on tea and coffee plantations and elsewhere—much higher than those endured by the generality of workers in imperialist countries—is a palpable, directly observable fact, experienced every day in the flesh by hundreds of millions of workers in low-wage countries. We don't need a theory to know this, we only need to remove our blinkers and open our eyes. But we *do* need a theory if we are to understand what we can see and work out the consequences that flow from this.

There is nothing empiricist about this argument. It does not contradict the fundamental postulate of Marx's law of value that the wage-form veils the intrinsically exploitative relation between capitalist and worker, or the principle of materialist dialectics that opposition between essence and appearance is a law of all dynamic systems containing contradiction.[1] What makes imperialism and super-exploitation *immediately* visible—even if what's visible is only the tip of the iceberg—is precisely *the systematic violation* of the law of value, and this is rooted in *the systematic violation of equality between proletarians.*

In the era of globalized production, even more than in previous stages of capitalism's imperialist evolution, workers are *not* equally mobile and are *not* equally free to sell their labour power to the highest bidder. Removal of impediments to cross-border flows of commodities and capital has spurred the migration of production to low-wage countries, but militarized borders and rising xenophobia have had the opposite effect on the migration of workers from these countries—not stopping it altogether, but inhibiting its flow and reinforcing migrants' vulnerable, second-class status. And so, factories freely cross the US–Mexican border and pass with ease through the walls of Fortress Europe, as do the commodities produced in them and the capitalists who own them, but the human beings who work in them have no right of passage. This is a travesty of globalization—a world without borders to everything and everyone except for working people.

Global wage differentials, in large measure resulting from suppression of the free movement of labour, provide a distorted reflection of global differences in the rate of exploitation (simply, the difference between the value generated by workers and what they are paid in wages). The Southward shift of production signifies

1 'Vemos cotidianamente "salir" el sol, hacer un recorrido por sobre la tierra, para luego ocultarse. Sabemos, no por lo que vemos, sino por conocimientos, que no es el sol el que gira alrededor de la tierra, sino al revés. [Every day we see the sun 'rise', make a tour of the land, and then hide. We know, not by what we see, but by knowledge, that it is not the sun that rotates around the Earth, but the other way round.—*Ed.*]' (Osorio 2019, p. 2)

that the profits of firms headquartered in Europe, North America and Japan, the value of all manner of financial assets derived from these profits, and the living standards of the citizens of these nations have become highly dependent on the higher rates of exploitation of workers in so-called 'emerging nations'. Neoliberal globalization must therefore be recognized as a new, imperialist stage of capitalist development, where imperialism is defined by its economic essence: the exploitation of Southern living labour by Northern capitalists.

Instead of supersession of imperialism and convergence between 'developed' and eternally 'developing' countries, imperialism is today manifested in an apartheid-like global system of racism, national oppression, cultural humiliation, militarism and state violence that systematically denies citizenship and basic human rights to the workers and farmers of the South and has turned Southern nations into reserves of super-exploitable labour-power for transnational corporations and their local agents.

None of this is hidden from view. The exploitative character of apartheid capitalism in South Africa was apparent to all with eyes to see, and this is no less true of twenty-first century imperialist capitalism. The systematic violation of equality between proletarians profoundly affects the global operation of the law of value—how could it be otherwise, given that value relations are social relations? The systematic violation of equality between proletarians is incontrovertible, and so are the divergent rates of exploitation that *necessarily* flow from this. Yet many Marxists dogmatically insist that the value relations of the contemporary global economy are identical to those in the idealized marketplace analysed by Marx in his quest for a 'general theory' of capital, and that none of the simplifying assumptions he made to that end need to be relaxed.[2]

2 'Lo que es un supuesto para "el análisis general del capital", esto es, a nivel del modo de producción, es asumido por algunas corrientes marxistas como

Marx's theory provides the essential keys needed to reveal the exploitative and antagonistic relation that lies hidden behind the surface appearance of freedom and equality between buyer and seller. But what we have here is a perverse inversion of this: the use of Marx's theory not to reveal what is hidden, *but to throw a cloak over what is blindingly obvious to any untutored but unprejudiced observer.*

Marxist imperialism-denial comes in different flavours. William Robinson and David Harvey openly declare that the age of imperialism is over and that the term is obsolete. Many others avoid the subject as far as they can, and when they can't, they avoid referring to imperialism by name, preferring anodyne euphemisms like 'core and periphery' or 'developed and developing'. And there are those who continue to describe the global capitalist economy and its leading firms and nations as imperialist, but evacuate this term of its content and meaning, reserving the term for inter-state relations while denying that imperialism has anything to do with international differences in the rate of exploitation.

'The Global Class War', an article in the journal *Catalyst*, is a recent example of the last of these trends. In it, Ramaa Vasudevan criticizes two recent books, including one by myself (Smith 2016), for acknowledging the actuality of *super-exploitation* and for seeking a theoretical concept of it.[3]

In her own words,

---

una ley de hierro. Se asume con esto que el supuesto debe prevalecer en el capitalismo en todo nivel de análisis, en todo lugar o espacio, y en todo tiempo. [What is an assumption for 'the general analysis of capital', that is, at the level of the mode of production, is assumed by some Marxist currents as an iron law. This assumes that the assumption must prevail in capitalism at all levels of analysis, in all places or spaces, and at all times.—*Ed.*]' (Osorio 2018, p. 157)

[3] The other book critiqued by Vasudevan is Samir Amin's *Modern Imperialism, Monopoly Finance Capital, and Marx's Law of Value.*

> [An] argument … has been put forward recently … that the advanced capitalist countries extract imperialist superprofits by subjecting workers in the periphery to super-exploitation. US imperialism in these formulations systematically subjects workers in the US and workers in Bangladesh, China, and Mexico to *different* rates of exploitation. The US worker faces a lower rate of exploitation, and this lower rate hinges on the super-exploitation of workers in the latter countries. Instead of workers across the world finding common cause against the onslaught of capital, these arguments place workers in the US and workers in the periphery in structurally separate positions, and also implicate US workers in the mechanisms of imperialist rents. (Vasudevan 2019, p. 112)

Despite its imprecision ('hinges on', 'structurally separate' and 'mechanisms of imperialist rent' are open to different interpretations); taking 'US' to mean 'US and other imperialist countries'; with the proviso that 'workers in Bangladesh, China', etc. refers specifically to the half-a-billion-or-so of them who work in low-wage rungs of global value chains; and with the addition that this global iteration of divide-and-conquer has very different dynamics in times of crisis, as now, this fairly summarizes my view. What does she counterpose to this?

> As US-led corporate capital spreads and tightens its web of control across borders to directly or indirectly exploit lower-wage workers in Latin America, Asia, and Africa, it has at its disposal a significantly larger pool of labour from which surplus value can be extracted and claimed. The access to this vast and growing global pool of labour, and the heightening competition between workers in this pool, enables US corporate capital to raise the overall rate of exploitation. This is the true significance of the global expansion of US corporate

capital and global labour arbitrage. (Vasudevan 2019, p. 130)

What is 'the overall rate of exploitation'? Does she mean the global average? If so, this implies that the rate of exploitation differs around the world. Or does she mean that there is only one 'overall rate of exploitation', and any deviations from it are minuscule and insignificant? Vasudevan dodges these obvious questions, though the following passage suggests that she believes in the second option:

> The proponents of the super-exploitation thesis are right to point to the absolute degradation of the lives and livelihoods of working people in the periphery. They are also right to call attention to the impact of the expansion of the global reserve army of labour at the service of corporate capital. But the real significance of the globalization of capital is that it has buttressed a hike in the *global* rate of exploitation.[4] (Vasudevan 2019, p. 135)

In other words, if workers in Bangladeshi garment factories or Chinese production lines are subject to a higher rate of exploitation than workers in imperialist countries, this has no significance. Whether those workers whose integration into global value chains is responsible for this increase are also subject to a higher rate of exploitation is arbitrarily excluded from consideration. Indeed, to even ask questions about this is 'to pit the interests of low-wage workers in the periphery against those in the United States' (Vasudevan 2019, p. 110).[5]

This is a curious argument. By the same logic, we should not inquire into gender inequality, for fear of pitting the interests of women against men; nor should we acknowledge racial

[4] All emphases in cited passages are in the original, unless otherwise stated.

[5] This quote is from the epigraph prefacing Vasudevan's article. It is not clear whether the words were authored by *Catalyst* editors or by Vasudevan.

discrimination, for fear of pitting Black against White—even though the violation of equality between workers resulting from imperialist divide-and-conquer, as measured by differences in the price of labour-power, is very much more severe than that which results from racism and women's oppression within countries (and racism, of course, is fundamentally an expression of imperialism).[6] Communists must, by definition, bring to the fore the common interests of all workers, but this can only be done by acknowledging the divisions that exist, and that these divisions are not purely ideological but have material substance.

Why does Vasudevan refuse to acknowledge such blindingly obvious facts? Because she fears the implications: that the two groups of workers are indeed in 'structurally separate positions', and that workers in imperialist countries are somehow 'implicated in the mechanisms of imperialist rents'. Despite her fears, these facts do *not* contradict the view that workers in all parts of the world are locked in a 'global race to the bottom', nor do they mean that socialist revolution is impossible in the USA, UK and other imperialist countries.[7] But recognition of these facts does help us to understand why the revolutionary road is so difficult, and why

6 It is not my intention to make a glib comparison between imperialist oppression and women's oppression, which in any case cannot be measured by relative access to material goods. It is true that women contribute vast amounts of unpaid domestic labour—but the relevant point here is that consumption levels, access to health and education, etc., depend much more on nationality than gender.

7 Some who do acknowledge these facts (e.g. Cope 2019; Amin 2018) have concluded otherwise. In my opinion, their conclusions are overly pessimistic because they fail to acknowledge the potential consequences and implications which flow from the current crisis of capitalism, still in its early stages, which is the most profound crisis it has ever faced; they fail to acknowledge how the working class within imperialist countries has been transformed by migration and by the massive influx of women into its ranks; and they underestimate the potential for revolutionary advances in Southern nations to foster the emergence of revolutionary internationalism within the imperialist countries.

the spontaneous economic struggle—the attempt by workers to defend or improve their position within capitalism,

> leads precisely to its subordination to bourgeois ideology ... The spontaneous working-class movement is trade unionism ... and trade-unionism means the ideological enslavement of the workers by the bourgeoisie. Hence our task ... is *to combat spontaneity, to divert* the working-class movement from the spontaneous, trade unionist striving to come under the wing of the bourgeoisie, and to bring it under the wing of revolutionary Social-Democracy. (Lenin [1902] 1978, p. 50)

BOURGEOIS VS MARXIST CONCEPTIONS OF PRODUCTIVITY

Vasudevan's imperialism-denial differs from that of her co-thinkers in one important respect. While she avoids expressing an opinion on whether or not higher rates of exploitation are prevalent in low-wage countries, others are not so coy.

Nigel Harris (1986, pp. 119–20) expressed the consensus opinion of Marxist opponents of dependency theory as follows[8]: 'Other things being equal, the higher the productivity of labour, the higher the income paid to the worker (since his or her reproduction costs are higher) and the more exploited he or she is—that is, the greater the proportion of the worker's output [that] is appropriated by the employer.'

[8] 'Dependency' is a euphemism for imperialism, a concession made to the desire of the national bourgeoisie and 'modernizing elites' of subject nations for independent capitalist development, and to the falsely named 'communist' parties who sought to bloc with them on this basis. The term has now passed into history and cannot be rewritten, but it can be and is being filled with new revolutionary content, especially in the lively and fast-expanding renaissance of Marxism and dependency theory in Latin America.

Expanding on this, Alex Callinicos (2009) argued that

> A highly paid worker may well be more exploited than a low paid worker because the former produces, relative to his wages, a larger amount of surplus value than the latter does. There is indeed reason to believe that the generally higher wages paid to Western workers reflect the greater costs of their reproduction; but the expenditure in particular on education and training which forms part of these costs creates a more highly skilled workforce which is therefore more productive *and more exploited* than its Third World counterparts. [My emphasis]

Callinicos's argument contains two major errors. First, given that all but the highest-paid workers spend all of their wages on consumption goods, 'wage' and 'cost of reproduction' are synonymous, and this part of Callinicos's argument is both tautological and banal. He does not ask *why* the cost of reproduction of labour-power is so much higher in imperialist countries than elsewhere. If he did, he would have to consider that higher wages, pensions, free healthcare, etc., may, at least in part, be explained by class struggle within imperialist countries pressing the exploiters to make concessions—but this would imply a lower rate of exploitation than in those countries where workers' economic struggles are met with machine guns and military dictatorships. So, he chooses not to ask the question; instead he argues that grotesque wage differentials between imperialist countries and those they exploit and oppress are normal and natural consequences of uneven development.

That's bad enough, but his second error is much more serious. He argues that differences in the productivity of workers in 'Western' countries compared to those in nations they dominate is even greater than differences in their wages, with the result that the rate of exploitation is higher there than in low-wage countries. In the quote above, Callinicos places the emphasis on the allegedly much higher skill of workers in imperialist countries, though why US and UK assembly-line workers, nurses, truck drivers, etc., should be so much more skilled than their homologues in Mexico and China is hard to fathom. He and his co-thinkers should ponder the wisdom of Marx:

> The distinction between skilled and unskilled labour rests in part on pure illusion, or, to say the least, on distinctions that have long since ceased to be real, and that survive only by virtue of a traditional convention; in part on the helpless condition of some groups of the working class, a condition that prevents them from exacting equally with the rest the value of their labour-power. (Marx [1867] 2010a, p. 208)

The emphasis Callinicos places on qualified labour has its intellectual roots in the work of Michael Kidron, one of the founders of the 'International Socialist Tendency' to which Callinicos, Harris and Vasudevan belong. Kidron (1974, p. 100) argued,

> If there is one outstanding difference between [British and Indian workers] it lies in the different degrees to which they are culturally enriched. The average British worker can be expected to read and drive; he or she will normally be able to handle a wide range of tools and concepts and respond to a wide range of stimuli on the basis of knowledge rather than from personal experience. The Indian worker will not. . . .
>
> The cost of maintaining them effectively—their value—is bound to reflect this difference. For example, a truck driver dare not make a practice of sleeping at the wheel and must therefore be able to ensure rest at home and a home to rest

> in; a bullock-cart driver dares and often does nod off, so his housing is less important to the employer … and his wage will not need to contain as large a housing component. New entrants into a factory in Britain need to be able to read, and their parents' wages need to contain therefore a child-support and -education component. New mill hands in India need not, and usually do not, read, so the pressure on their parents' wages is less. And so on and on.

Kidron's argument is not only repugnant chauvinism (especially his outrageous claim that Indian workers, unlike British workers, are unable to think in concepts), it is also nonsense. Indian truck-drivers arguably need to be *more* alert and skilful than their British counterparts—because they are more likely to have to dodge bullocks and potholes as they transport their loads. Indian 'mill hands' are likely to have more children and an extended family to support, and their wage will have to cover their healthcare and education, unlike in Britain, where these services are provided *gratis* by the state.

Most attempts to deny imperialist super-exploitation by pointing to the higher productivity of workers in imperialist countries place emphasis on the more advanced and capital-intensive means of production (which is often accompanied by deskilling). For example, Charles Bettelheim, who, in his critique of Arghiri Emmanuel's *Unequal Exchange* (Bettelheim 1972, p. 302), argued that 'the more the productive forces are developed, the more the proletarians are exploited'. This view has been repeated countless times by avowed Marxists, for example Claudio Katz, who wrote 'la tasa de plusvalía es superior en el centro. Allí se concentran las inversiones más significativas y se gesta el mayor volumen de trabajo excedente … la magnitud del trabajo confiscado es claramente superior en las economías más productivas del centro [… the rate of surplus-value is higher in the centre. The most significant investments are concentrated there and the greatest volume of surplus-labour is generated … the magnitude of the confiscated work is clearly higher in the most productive economies of the centre]' (Katz 2017, p. 10).[9]

This widely-held view is confounded by a simple fact: the goods consumed by workers in the North are no longer produced solely or mainly in the North; to an ever-greater extent, they are produced by low-wage labour in the Global South. *Their* productivity, *their* wages significantly substantially determine the value of the basket of consumption goods that reproduces labour-power in imperialist countries, and therefore the value of this labour power.

But this only deals with the value *of* labour-power—*v*, the denominator in s/v, Marx's deceptively simple formula for the rate of exploitation. The value *generated by* this labour power, once *v* has been subtracted, provides *s*, the numerator. When we turn to examine how much wealth is generated by the expenditure of a given quantity of labour-power, we discover that the view of Callinicos, Bettelheim, Katz, etc., suffers from a much deeper problem: it is premised on a bourgeois concept of productivity, one that is antithetical to Marx's theory of value.

Marx counted among the greatest of his discoveries '*the two-fold character of labour according to whether it is expressed in use-value or exchange-value*' (Marx [1867] 2010c, p. 407).[10] To the

9 He claims that Marini 'always' agreed with this, and he also claims that 'este diagnóstico es aceptado también por los defensores contemporáneos del concepto de superexplotación [this diagnosis is also accepted by contemporary defenders of the concept of super-exploitation—*Ed.*]'. Unfortunately, he does not support these assertions with a single quotation from any of the sources he cites.

10 The sentence from which this came: 'The best points in my book are: 1. (this is fundamental to all understanding of the FACTS) the *two-fold character of labour* according to whether it is expressed in use-value or exchange-value … 2. the treatment of *surplus-value regardless of its particular* forms as profit, interest, ground rent, etc.'

two-fold character of labour there corresponds to the two-fold character of the productivity of labour: the universal definition of labour productivity, true for human society in all its stages of development, is the quantity of use-values that can be produced by a day or a week of living labour. But for capitalists the production of use-values is only a means to a very different end, the production of exchange-value. From this flows an entirely different and quintessentially bourgeois concept and measure of productivity: how much the firm's 'value-added' (the market value of the firm's output minus the market value of all inputs) is increased by one hour, day, or week, etc., of labour.

Measured in terms of use-values, workers are today vastly more productive than, say, a hundred years ago. But in terms of exchange value, *no comparison whatsoever can be made between today and one hundred years ago*, since the products of today's living labour are only compared *in reality* with other products of today's living labour. Higher capital composition raises labour productivity—*of use-values*, but makes *no difference whatsoever* to generation of exchange-value. (I leave aside the special case of individual capitals which possess a temporary monopoly over a more advanced production technique.) This is what Callinicos, Katz et al. do not understand; they believe that workers in high-tech (i.e. capital intensive) industries produce more value and are therefore more exploited than workers in low-tech industries, even within a single nation. This flatly contradicts Marx, who 'assume[d] that the level of exploitation of labour, or the rate of surplus-value, is the same ... [in] capitals that set in motion unequal amounts of living labour [i.e. whether they are capital-intensive or labour-intensive]'; and this assumption in turn rests on 'competition among workers, and an equalization that takes place by their constant migration between one sphere of production and another' (Marx [1894] 2010b, p. 173).

Assuming labour-power of average intensity, and assuming

that it is exchanged for the same wage, and leaving to one side the issue of qualified or complex labour, the new value generated by a given quantity of it *is wholly independent of the organic composition of the capital it sets in motion*. In other words, again assuming both labours are of average intensity and assuming they are paid the same wages, the quantity of value produced in a standard working day by the hamburger-flipper standing in the car park of a steel factory is *the same* as that produced during the same time by the steelworker inside that factory.

The apparently higher productivity of workers in capital-intensive branches of production is an illusion created by transfers of value from labour-intensive branches of production. What the capitalist thinks of as profits magically appearing out of dead labour, i.e. from his machinery and other inputs, is in fact value created by living labour employed by rival capitalists with lower organic compositions. When Marxists argue that workers in capital-intensive industries produce more value than those in labour-intensive industries, as do the opponents of dependency theory considered here, they are thinking in bourgeois concepts, no matter how much they dress them up in Marxist verbiage.

To conclude this discussion of bourgeois versus Marxist conceptions of productivity, let us now imagine that, because of superior trade-union organization, the steelworker receives a higher wage than the fast-food worker who produces her/his lunch. With all other assumptions still in place, the fast-food worker now endures a higher rate of exploitation than the steelworker s/he serves. All of this should be elementary to anyone who is versed in the basic principles of Marx's law of value. So why do so many Marxists have such difficulty understanding what happens when the workers who produce our steelworkers' consumption goods are located not in the steel mills' car park but in another country? Readers can work out their own answer to this question, but one contributory factor is errors and omissions in Marx's great work.

IMPERIALISM AND MARX'S *CAPITAL*

Marx, in continuation of the last-cited passage, said that 'in theory, we assume that the laws of capitalist mode of production develop in their pure form. In reality, this is only an approximation; but the approximation is all the more exact, the more the capitalist mode of production is developed and the less it is adulterated by survivals of earlier economic conditions with which it is amalgamated'.[11]

We now know that Marx was wrong about this. He wrote eloquently about why imperialism was a necessary condition for the rise of capitalism, but he failed to anticipate how capitalism's imperialist evolution would result in *the oppression of nations becoming an intrinsic property of the capital–labour relation itself.* As Andy Higginbottom has pointed out,

> The wage labour relation is not only between capital and labour, but between northern capital and southern labour. In this sense, class exploitation and racial or national oppression are fused ... The working class of the oppressed nations/Third World/global South is systematically paid below the value of labour power of the working class of the oppressor nations/First World/global North. This is not because the southern working class produces less value, but because it is more oppressed and more exploited. (Higginbottom 2011, p. 284)

[11] This argument is elaborated in great depth in *Capital*, vol. 1, where Marx says 'a working day of given length always creates the same amount of value, *no matter how the productiveness of labour*, and, with it, the mass of the product, and the price of each single commodity produced, *may vary*. If the value created by a working day of 12 hours be, say, six shillings, then, although the mass of the articles produced varies with the productiveness of labour, the only result is that the value represented by six shillings is spread over a greater or less number of articles' (Marx [1867] 2010a, p. 520).

This is the fundamental reason why Marx's *Capital* does not contain a theory of super-exploitation, or (which is the same thing) a theory of imperialism; a lacuna which cannot be explained solely or mainly by a decision to leave these matters to a volume of *Capital* that he never got around to writing. Whether or not Marx could have anticipated this qualitatively new stage in the evolution of the capital–labour relation is open to debate. The exceptional importance of Ruy Mauro Marini's contribution to the Marxist theory of imperialism lies, in part, in his observation that, *during Karl Marx's own lifetime*, imports of cheaper food and other consumption goods produced by super-exploited labour in Britain's colonies and neo-colonies helped increase relative surplus-value within Britain itself, reducing necessary labour-time without lowering consumption levels. Higginbottom points out that

> Marini places the necessity of super-exploitation of labour in the mid-nineteenth century, that is, before the appearance of modern imperialism as a world system as portrayed by Lenin. The transition in England from production dominated by methods of absolute surplus to relative surplus-value depended on cheap imports as well as greater productivity. . . . Marini's work shows that Marx was not correct on every point, even in his own time.[12] (Higginbottom 2014, pp. 31–32)

Marx's error, 150 years later, *has still not been corrected.* Its correction will critically determine whether or not the Renaissance of Marxism—on which the future of humanity rests—is stillborn. *Yes! It really is that important!*

We, of course, have the great advantage of hindsight. In

[12] As Amanda Latimer (2016) has pointed out, 'Marini's work undermines [the] myth that the shift to relative surplus-value in England was entirely the product of *national* class struggle'.

mitigation of Marx, if not in exoneration, we should recall a fundamental premise of materialist dialectics: there cannot be a concrete concept of a system of interaction that is not itself fully concrete and developed. Just as Karl Marx could not have written *Capital* before capitalism's mature, fully-evolved form had come into existence with the rise of industrial capitalism in England, so it is unreasonable to expect to find, in his writings or in those of Lenin and others writing at the time of the birth of capitalism's imperialist stage, a theory of imperialism that is able to explain its fully-evolved modern form. And Marx not only provided theoretical foundations for a theory of the imperialist form of the law of value, he provided copious clues and insights that point in this direction—although today's imperialism-denying 'Marxists' pay as much attention to them as today's 'Christians' do to Jesus's words about the obstacles in the way of rich men entering the kingdom of heaven. This analogy is apt—our imperialism-denying Marxists treat *Capital* like a sacred text, yet ignore what they find uncomfortable in it.

In Volume 1 of *Capital*, Marx analysed in great depth and detail two ways in which capitalists strive to increase the rate of exploitation. One is by lengthening the working day, thereby increasing absolute surplus-value; and the other is to increase relative surplus-value by increasing the productivity of workers producing consumption goods, thereby reducing necessary labour-time. In numerous places he briefly describes a third, as in the chapter entitled 'The Concept of Relative Surplus Value', where he writes: 'The duration of the surplus-labour . . . [could be extended] only by lowering the wages of the labourer below the value of his labour-power. . . . Despite the important part which this method plays in actual practice, we are excluded from considering it in this place, by our assumption, that all commodities, including labour-power, are bought and sold at their full value' (Marx [1867] 2010a, pp. 318–19).

Pushing the wage of the worker down below the value of his labour-power, that is, super-exploitation—a narrow definition, since it assumes an idealized, unitary economy where labour-power has a single value—is again mentioned two chapters later, during a discussion of the consequences for workers when 'machinery ... gradually seizes control of the whole of a given field of production', with the result that a 'section of the working class ... rendered superfluous by machinery ... swamps the labour-market, and makes the price of labour-power fall below its value' (ibid., p. 557). Here, Marx is talking about the episodic, sectoral unemployment arising from the mechanization of a new branch of industry, but its relevance to the modern era hardly needs stating. A huge section of the working class in the Global South has been rendered superfluous by the inability of modern production methods to soak up enough labour to prevent rising unemployment, and this alone, even before we take into account the violent suppression of the free movement of labour and the much harsher labour regimes and political repression prevalent in low-wage countries, exerts a powerful force causing the price of their labour-power to fall below its value. Even before we establish the precise connection between the wage, the value of labour-power and the rate of exploitation, this already constitutes *prima facie* evidence that the value of labour-power has been forced down much more cruelly in Southern than in Northern nations, *so much so as to force a permanently lower value of labour-power upon these workers.* It is also powerful evidence that wage differentials are determined, in large part, by factors that are quite independent of the workers' productivity when at work, such as absence of social security, structural unemployment, and repressive labour regimes.

Not only did Marx leave to one side the reduction of wages below their value, he made a further abstraction that, though necessary for his general analysis of capital, must also be relaxed if we are to analyse capitalism's current stage of development: 'The difference in the rates of surplus-value in different countries, and consequently the national differences in the degree of exploitation of labour, are immaterial for our present analysis' (Marx [1894] 2010b, p. 142). So, two elements that are crucial to a theory of contemporary imperialism—international variations in the value of labour-power and in the rate of exploitation—were explicitly excluded by Marx from his general theory as elaborated in *Capital*. Anwar Shaikh was therefore wrong to contend that 'the development of the law of value in *Capital* contains all the necessary elements for its extension to international exchange' (Shaikh 1980, p. 208).

RATE OF EXPLOITATION; RATE OF SURPLUS-VALUE

Throughout this essay, 'rate of surplus-value' is synonymous with and interchangeable with 'rate of exploitation'. But this identity only holds if we make several major simplifications.

First, it requires that we exclude the distinction between productive and non-productive labour. Security guards, bank clerks and other non-productive workers produce neither value nor surplus-value, so it is inappropriate to talk of the rate of surplus-value in these cases. Yet their working day is still divided between necessary labour—the time required to replace the socially-necessary labour-time embodied in their basket of consumption goods (i.e. the value of their labour power, v)—and surplus-labour (the amount by which their working day exceeds v). Two important conclusions follow from this. First, all workers who contribute more labour than they receive in the form of consumption goods are exploited, irrespective of whether their surplus-labour is used for production or non-production tasks, or even if it is squandered. Second, all workers are exploited—except those who receive a super-wage—but not all of them generate surplus-value. It necessarily follows that, once we take into account the distinction between production and non-production labour, the average rate of surplus-value of production workers is greater than the average rate of exploitation of all workers.

Second, 'rate of surplus-value' applies only to living labour employed by a capitalist to produce commodities, either because he has bought this living labour for a wage or because he owns the labourer,[13] as in capitalist employment of slaves (Higginbottom 2018). Self-employed workers do not produce surplus-value; if they receive less than the value of their product then they undergo unequal exchange. Capitalistically employed workers make up the overwhelming majority of the economically active population in imperialist countries, but this is not so in most countries in Africa, Asia and Latin America. As Paul Sweezy pointed out,

> The rate of exploitation is and always has been vastly higher in the periphery than in the centre. In the centre, the rate of exploitation is for all practical purposes the same as the rate of surplus-value.[14] This is not so of the periphery, where only a small part of the workforce is employed as wage labourers in capitalist industry, with a much larger proportion being exploited directly and indirectly by landlords, traders, and usurers, primarily in the countryside but also in the cities and towns. Here all or most of the surplus extorted from the workers not employed in capitalist industry is commercialized and becomes indistinguishably mingled with capitalistically produced surplus-value. In these circumstances we can speak of a social rate of exploitation but should not confuse

[13] I refer to the owners of capital as 'he', reflecting the overwhelming concentration of wealth and power in male hands and the more general oppression of women intrinsic to capitalism. Otherwise, I use 's/he'.

[14] As in his other writings, Sweezy disregards the distinction between productive and non-productive labour, a distinction which is arguably much more important in developed imperialist countries than in their colonies and neo-colonies.

> the concept with a rate of surplus-value in the usual sense. (Sweezy 1981, p. 76)

In continuation, he says (in an argument that has much in common with Marini's thesis) that the higher rate of exploitation in subject nations allows 'local ruling classes and allied elites to live on a level compatible to that of the bourgeoisies of the centre, while at the same time making possible a massive flow of monetized surplus product (in the form of profits, interest, rents, royalties, etc.) from periphery to centre'. He adds,

> The counterpart of the very high (and frequently rising) rate of exploitation in the periphery is a lower (and over time relatively stable) rate of surplus-value in the centre. There are two basic and interrelated reasons for this. On the one hand, the working class of the centre is more highly developed and is in a better position to organize and struggle for its own interests. On the other hand, the bourgeoisies of the centre learn through historical experience that a situation that allows the standard of living of the proletariat to rise over time (a stable rate of surplus-value combined with rising productivity) is not only functional but even indispensable for the operation of the system as a whole.

MONOPOLY AND SUPER-EXPLOITATION

Before we burrow deeper into the nature of capitalist exploitation and imperialist super-exploitation, it is useful to consider how these two closely-related categories stand in relation to another essential constitutive element of capitalism: monopoly. Monopoly is inscribed in the DNA of capitalism—individual capitalists don't so much strive to compete as to find a way of avoiding competition, to get an edge over rivals, to exercise some form of monopoly that will give them higher than average profits. The law of value—which, in its simplest form, explains that commodities freely bought and sold sell at their value—results from the incessant efforts of individual capitalists to violate this law. Their wild compulsion can only be contained by an external force, hence the necessity for a State and system of laws independent of individual capitalists—and hence, too, the ceaseless attempts of individual capitalists and groups of capitalists to capture the State in order to satiate their hunger for monopoly profits.

Monopoly comes in many forms. Some pertain to *production*, e.g. technological innovations that allow an individual capitalist to produce a given commodity more efficiently than others; others to *distribution* (branding or other forms of monopoly in the marketplace, such as barriers to new entrants, State capture, privileged access to cheap inputs, etc.); all may be short-lived or long-lasting. To each instance of monopoly there corresponds a rent, an unearned income, an extra profit at the expense of lower profits for the rest. Monopoly, therefore, *redistributes* surplus-value between capitals, *but makes no addition to it.*

This is even true of technological innovations that reduce the quantity of labour required to produce workers' consumption goods. Only when this innovation becomes generalized, i.e. when it ceases to be monopolized by an individual capitalist, in other words when it ceases to be an innovation, does it result in a lowering of the value of labour-power and a corresponding rise in the rate of surplus-value—and only then if none of these gains are captured by workers through higher real wages.

While monopoly is all about the *distribution* of surplus-value, exploitation is all about its *extraction*. And just as every capitalist dreams of becoming a monopolist, so it is in the DNA of every capitalist to seek ways to maximize the extraction of surplus-value. As we have just seen, in *Capital*, Marx analyses in detail two ways in which capitalists do this—*by extending the working day* beyond 'necessary labour-time', i.e. the time needed to replace the values consumed by the worker and her/his family—which Marx called *absolute* surplus-value; and by changing the ratio between necessary labour-time and surplus labour-time within an unchanged working day via productivity advances that cheapen workers' consumption goods—which he called *relative* surplus-value. *Both are entirely distinct from the reduction of necessary labour-time through* 'pushing the wage of the worker down below the value of his labour-power' (see p. 50 for the rest of quote)—the standard definition of super-exploitation, critiqued later in this essay.

It follows from the above that imperialist rent and imperialist super-exploitation are conceptually distinct, even if in reality they are intimately related. Samir Amin was therefore in error to conflate the two: 'the visible part of imperialist rent . . . arises from the grade scaling of labour-power prices . . . The submerged part of the rent [arises from] access to the planet's resources' (Amin 2018, p. 110).

We can now put the two constitutive elements of capitalism—monopoly/competition and exploitation/super-exploitation—together. Every capitalist dreams of becoming a monopolist, but for capitalists in Vietnam, Cambodia, Mexico and other Southern nations their dreams remain just that, dreams; they have no choice but to rely exclusively on the extraction of surplus-value from their own workers by super-exploiting them up to and beyond the limits—or rather, to sate themselves on what's left after monopolists and imperialists have taken their share. (China is an extremely important but as yet partial exception to this, which is why it is on a collision course with incumbent imperialist powers, principally Japan and the United States.) In contrast, imperialist monopoly capital does have the option of sharing some of its monopoly rents and imperial rents with its own workers—to buy social peace, to expand the market for its goods, and also to finance State expenditure on hard and soft power in order to reinforce its imperialist domination over subject nations.

If Marx's concepts of absolute and relative surplus-value are insufficient to explain the realities of exploitation in contemporary global production networks, what else do we need? In a nutshell—*a theoretical concept of super-exploitation.* But before we can conceptualize super-exploitation, we need a deeper, richer concept of exploitation.

THE MARXIST THEORY OF EXPLOITATION (I) —THE VALUE *OF* LABOUR-POWER

The seemingly simple formula for the rate of exploitation, s/v, is, on closer examination, anything but simple. The value *of* labour-power and the value *generated by* it are far more different from each other than is usually supposed. The fact that both the numerator and the denominator of s/v can be expressed as simple numbers, each expressing two parts of the same working day—with the rate of exploitation given by the simple ratio between them—leads many to forget just how extremely different from each other they in fact are. This becomes clear when we ask two elementary questions. What determines the value *of* labour-power? What determines the value *generated by* labour-power?

Taking these questions in turn, the determinants of the value of labour-power can be distilled into seven elements:

1) the fecundity of nature, i.e. the ready availability of food, building materials; and its hospitability—the need for protection against the elements, etc. For example, if it takes longer to catch fish, the value of labour-power that depends on them for sustenance must rise if consumption levels are to stay the same;
2) the proportion of use-values required for the reproduction of labour-power that are freely provided by domestic labour, the non-capitalist economy, etc.;

3) the productivity of labour *in branches of the capitalist economy that produce workers' consumption goods*;
4) the incidence of super-exploitation in those branches;
5) the size of the so-called 'moral and historical' component of the value of labour-power, i.e. the extent to which the class struggle and general social evolution (different ways of saying the same thing) has resulted in the incorporation of new needs into those necessary for the reproduction of labour-power;
6) the average degree of complexity/qualification of labour within a national economy, which is closely related to its productive structure, but which is also related to the 'moral and historical' element listed above;
7) the intensity of oppression and subjugation of workers in a given national economy, including the ferocity of employer/State repression, the degree of unity/disunity of the working class, the structural scarcity or super-abundance of labour-power, border controls suppressing the free mobility of labour.

Each of the determinants of the value of labour-power requires a chapter to itself, and each lends itself to empirical research as well as theoretical reflection. Here we only have space for the briefest discussion.

None of these factors, not even the first, are purely endogenous—consider, for example, the consequences for hundreds of millions of working people across the Global South of over-fishing by imperialist fishing fleets, or the impact of imperialism-engendered climate change on nature's fecundity and hospitability.

The second factor listed, i.e. the strength of patriarchy, the size of the non-capitalist economy, etc., is fundamentally a consequence of imperialism, of its 'development of underdevelopment'.

The third factor has undergone an enormous transformation during the neoliberal era, with the massive relocation of industries producing workers' consumption goods to low-wage countries.

The fourth factor must be considered in tandem with the third—the value of labour-power is determined not only by the productivity of workers employed in the production of consumption goods, but also the degree to which they are super-exploited. Sweatshop production cheapens these commodities and lowers the value of labour-power that depends on them.

The fifth factor, the 'moral and historical' element, is determined by class struggle, and this takes place at a national *and* an international level. What workers succeed in incorporating into the value of their labour-power in any one country is the result of global class struggle, not just the struggle within that particular country. For example, it was rising national liberation struggles in Britain's colonies and neo-colonies—not just the social reform movement at home—that convinced its imperialist rulers to concede free healthcare and education to Britain's workers after the Second World War. Their aim was not just to pacify workers by giving them what they want, but to forge a 'social contract' with leaders of their trade unions and the Labour Party—and thereby secure their active support for wars against insurgent peoples in its colonies and neo-colonies. On the other hand, even though workers outside of the imperialist countries have been excluded from enjoying these gains, they have nevertheless become progressively incorporated into what all workers considered to be their rights, their entitlements.

The sixth factor is also a function of imperialist development: a much higher proportion (though still a minority) of the working class in imperialist nations functions as complex/qualified labour than in dependent capitalism, but we must also remember Marx's warning that much of the distinction between skilled and unskilled labour rests on 'pure illusion' (see p. 42 for quote) as, for example, women fighting for equal pay have discovered.

The seventh factor, in sum, expresses the degree of national oppression endured by workers in a given nation, i.e. the degree to which their equality with workers elsewhere in the world is violated. It is argued here that in the neoliberal era this has become the most important factor of all, and is a key determinant of the fourth factor, whose importance has also vastly increased.

It is interesting to compare this list of factors determining the value of labour-power with one provided by Marx:

> The value of labour-power is determined by the value of the necessaries of life habitually required by the average labourer. The quantity of these necessaries is known at any given epoch of a given society, and can therefore be treated as a constant magnitude. What changes, is the value of this quantity. There are, besides, two other factors that enter into the determination of the value of labour-power. One, the expenses of developing that power, which expenses vary with the mode of production; the other, its natural diversity, the difference between the labour-power of men and women, of children and adults. (Marx [1867] 2010a, p. 519)

From this we can extract four factors; their correspondence with factors from among the seven as listed above is noted in parentheses at the end of each of them:

- The quantity of means of subsistence required by the average worker (1, 5, 6)
- The value of this quantity (i.e. the amount of socially-necessary labour required to produce it) (3, 4, 7)
- The cost of developing labour-power (i.e. its reproduction costs, including those of the worker's dependants) (2, 6)
- The natural diversity of labour-power (i.e. of men and women, children and adults): this is not applicable—I leave the labour-power of children out of the picture, and I dispute that there

is anything 'natural' about the value of male labour-power and female labour-power.

The differences between the two lists reflect the difference in the levels of abstraction deployed by Marx in his quest for a 'general theory' of capital and the aim of this work—a value theory of imperialism; and they also reflect the evolution of capitalism in the 150 years since Marx published Volume 1 of *Capital*. It is clear that many factors determine the value of labour-power and that their relative weight changes greatly from one historical period to another and from one country to another; all of which underlines why our concept of exploitation must be concrete, up-to-date and informed by empirical analysis, not just facilely lifted from Marx's *Capital* and mechanically applied to contemporary imperialist reality as if the transformations of the past one and a half centuries never happened.

THE MARXIST THEORY OF EXPLOITATION (II) —THE VALUE *GENERATED BY* LABOUR-POWER

Now we turn to consider the other element in the formula for the rate of exploitation—*s*. The law of value rests on a fundamental principle: 'the value which the labour-power produces . . . depends, not on its own value, but on the length of time it is in action' (Marx [1867] 2010a, p. 539). Furthermore, as we have seen above, it is also entirely independent of its value, of its productivity, and of the organic composition of the capital of which it is a part. Marx repeatedly stressed a fundamental principle in many places throughout his great work, for example,

> A working day of given length always creates the same amount of value, *no matter how the productiveness of labour*, and,

> with it, the mass of the product, and the price of each single commodity produced, *may vary*.
>
> If the value created by a working day of 12 hours be, say, six shillings, then, although the mass of the articles produced varies with the productiveness of labour, the only result is that the value represented by six shillings is spread over a greater or less number of articles. (Marx [1867] 2010a, p. 520; my emphasis)

What other factors, apart from duration, come into play? The intensity of labour is one—a worker working twice as fast as another will produce twice as much value in the same time. However, it is far from clear that workers in imperialist countries work with greater intensity than those in low-wage countries, and even if they do this is counterbalanced by the tendency for the working day and the working week to be much longer in low-wage countries. We can therefore leave this out of our analysis, and assume, as Marx himself did in the above quotation, that all living labour is expended with the same intensity.

Another is the degree of qualification or skill, discussed above when refuting the argument of Callinicos and Kidron that differences in the degree of qualification of labour-power between countries explain either the differences in wages between them or differences in the quantity of value they generate in a given period of time. For the reasons given, this too can be excluded from our 'concrete universal concept' (Ilyenkov 1960, pp. 84–88) of capitalist exploitation.

Yet another factor that must be considered is that the value generated by living labour is determined *ex post*, when the value of the commodities produced by this labour is realized through their sale:

> [T]he value of a commodity is determined not by the quantity of labour actually realized in it, but by the quantity of living labour necessary for its production. A commodity represents, say 6 working hours. If an invention is made by which it can be produced in 3 hours, the value, even of the commodity already produced, falls by half. (Marx [1867] 2010a, pp. 536–37)

This is an important and complex matter, yet it can be safely excluded from the current discussion for two reasons. First, while the *ex post* determination of value affects the rate of surplus-value and the rate of profit, it has no effect on the rate of exploitation (since the division of the working day into necessary labour and surplus-labour is unaffected by whether this labour-power is employed productively or not, whether it is squandered, or whether its products get sold). Second, it only comes into play when the productivity of labour advances; this will take place more or less rapidly in different branches of production and in different countries, and it is far from clear that productivity is advancing in imperialist countries faster than elsewhere—production outsourcing to low-wage countries has been an increasingly favoured alternative to boost profits than domestic investment in new, more productive technology.

Finally, we must consider the special case of workers employed by an individual capitalist who possesses a technical or technological innovation that allows him to produce a commodity more efficiently, i.e. more cheaply, than is the norm for that particular branch of production. Marx says: 'The exceptionally productive labour operates as intensified labour; it creates in equal periods of time greater values than average social labour of the same kind' (ibid., p. 435). On the face of it, this appears to contradict Marx's statement that 'variations in productivity have no impact whatever on the labour itself represented in value ... The same labour, therefore, performed for the same length of time, always yields the same amount of value, independently of any variations in productivity' (ibid., p. 137).

The contradiction between Marx's two statements is only apparent because, in the first of these quotes, Marx focuses on firm-specific levels of productivity while in the second of these quotes he abstracts from this. The different rates of surplus-value Marx talks about in the first quote deal exclusively with productivity differences between *individual firms* within a branch of production which produce identical commodities but in different amounts of time. To transpose these firm-specific productivity differences to differences between entire sectors with different organic compositions is a major error, a fundamental misreading of Marx's theory of value—yet this is exactly what imperialism-denying Marxists argue, so keen are they to 'prove' that workers in more advanced, capital-intensive industries produce more value per hour of their living labour, and that, by extension, workers in more advanced nations produce more value than those in underdeveloped nations, and are therefore just as exploited.

The unequal distribution of surplus-value is between capitalists 'in the same business', i.e. who produce the same commodities. The value which the more productive capitalist realizes upon the sale will capture an extra share of surplus-value *at the expense of* competitors whose productivity is lower than the average in that particular branch of production.[15] It should be clear that this only applies to individual capitals in direct competition with each other, and does not in any way imply that capitals in branches of production with higher organic compositions have a higher rate

[15] 'When Marx states that enterprises operating with below-average productivity obtain less than the average profit . . . all this . . . means is that the value or surplus-value actually produced by their workers is appropriated on the market by firms that function better. It does not at all mean that they have created less value or surplus-value than is indicated by the number of hours worked in them.' (Mandel 1975, p. 101)

of surplus-value than those in branches of production with lower organic compositions. I discuss this fascinating and important subject in more depth in *Imperialism in the Twenty-First Century* (2016, pp. 241–44), concluding as follows:

> [A]ssuming labour of average intensity and complexity ... *all* of the labour-power expended by workers employed in the less productive capitals counts *equally* toward total value, even if a disproportionate part of it is captured by the more productive capitalists. The more productive capitalists' extra profits derive not from their own more productive workers but from surplus-labour extracted from workers employed by technologically deficient capitals ... Thus the value generated by productive workers in a given amount of time is independent of their productivity, even if the value-added captured by their employers remains highly dependent on this. This is so fundamental, it must be repeated: a steelworker operating more technologically sophisticated machinery *does not* produce more exchange-value, s/he simply allows her/his capitalist employer to capture a larger share of it. It follows that the rate of exploitation—assuming equal wages, intensity of labour, etc.—is not higher in more productive capitals than in less productive capitals, as Euro-Marxist critics of dependency theory argue.

On the basis of the above simplifications and clarifications, it is clear that *none of the seven factors determining the value of labour-power discussed earlier have any bearing whatsoever on the value generated by it*. Even if we relax the simplifications and include intensity, qualification and *ex post* determination of value, it is clear that the determinants of the numerator and the denominator in the formula for the rate of exploitation have very little in common with each other, that our simple little formula, $^{s}/_{v}$, is far more complex than is generally supposed, and that references to the rate of exploitation that do not appropriately take this into account (Vasudevan, discussed above, provides a particularly crass example of this) is bad science.

THE MARXIST THEORY OF SUPER-EXPLOITATION

Earlier in this essay we saw many examples of the 'constant interweaving of the payment of labour-power by its value and below its value throughout *Capital* in its entirety' (Osorio 2018, p. 166). The way Marx posed the question—the 'reduction of wages below their value'—conformed to his 'general analysis of capital', in which he assumed a single unitary economy and perfect competition among capitalists and among workers, the condition for all commodities to sell at their value,[16] and for labour-power to have one, single, value. To conceptualize super-exploitation at the level not of 'capital in general' but of the contemporary global capitalist economy requires a significant modification to Marx's formulation: at the global level it is not so much a question of wages being above or below a common, single value, but of the value of labour-power, and not just its wage, being forced down in some countries but not in others.

In other words, what's crucial is not so much whether the value of labour-power is violated by under-remuneration, but, as stressed at the beginning of this essay, *whether the equality of workers is violated*, a violation that is reflected in their labour-powers having different values. Katz's attempt to 'correct' Marini's concept by affirming that labour-power has different values depending on where it resides, and that, because of this, 'the concept of payment of labour-power below its value should be substituted by lower remuneration of that

[16] Or rather, to sell at prices corresponding to the modified form of their value that Marx called 'prices of production'—prices consistent with the equalization of the rate of profit between different capitals.

resource' (Katz 2017, p. 10) gets us nowhere, for two reasons. First, if we accept (as we should) that the value of labour-power varies widely between different countries, the question that must then be answered is: *why does it vary so widely?* Second, Katz argues that this correction turns super-exploitation into a minor, non-systemic phenomenon that is just as likely to be encountered in 'core' countries as in the 'periphery'.[17] But this can only be true if we agree with his assertion that 'the magnitude of surplus-labour ... is clearly higher in the most productive economies of the centre' (ibid., p. 10). This is identical to the argument advanced by imperialism-denying Marxists discussed earlier in this essay, an argument rooted in conflation of use-value and exchange-value definitions of productivity. It is, in other words, nothing else than bourgeois economics dressed up as Marxist economics.

As we have seen, Marx repeatedly and explicitly excluded the suppression of wages below the value of labour-power from his 'general theory' of capital, each time repeatedly emphasizing the importance of this in real life. *Reduction in the value of labour-power by suppressing consumption levels* (or, what amounts to the same thing, shifting production to countries where consumption levels, and with them, the value of labour-power is much lower) *is a distinct, third way to increase surplus-value*,[18] and it has attained

[17] On this basis, Claudio Katz argued that 'dependency theory has no need for a concept of super-exploitation that was omitted by Marx' (Katz 2017, p. 15); Jaime Osorio replied that Katz's proposed 'reformulation of the Marxist theory of dependency is nothing else than a call for its repudiation' (Osorio 2018, p. 179).

[18] In *La Dialéctica de la Dependencia*, Marini argues: 'The concept of super-exploitation is not identical to that of absolute surplus-value since it also includes a type of production of relative surplus-value—that which corresponds to an increase in the intensity of labour. On the other hand, the conversion of part of the wages fund into a source of capital accumulation does not strictly represent a form of absolute surplus-value production, since it simultaneously affects both parts of the working day, not only of surplus labour-time as is the case with absolute surplus-value. Above all, super-exploitation is defined most of all by greater exploitation of the

incredible importance during the neoliberal era, becoming the driving force of its greatest transformation, the single-most important means of increasing the rate of surplus-value and countering the tendency of the rate of profit to fall.

Rediscovery of this third form of surplus-value is the breakthrough that makes it possible to apply the dynamic, scientific concepts contained in *Capital* to the concrete imperialist reality, and it was made by Andy Higginbottom in a 2009 conference paper entitled 'The Third Form of Surplus Value Increase', in which he built on the work of Marini and developed it further in a series of groundbreaking papers and articles, some of them cited in this essay. In his 2009 paper he said, 'Marx discusses three distinct ways that capital can increase surplus-value, but he names only two of these as absolute surplus-value and relative surplus-value. The third mechanism, reducing wages below the value of labour-power, Marx consigns to the sphere of competition and outside his analysis.' He develops this idea in later articles, for example where, criticizing the standard orthodox reading of *Capital*, he says:

> It is unclear … why lengthening the working day [absolute surplus-value], and the indirect, unintentional and mediated effect of increasing labour productivity on decreasing the value of labour-power [relative surplus-value] belong to the inner nature of capital, while capital directly decreasing wages does not. All three mechanisms increase the rate of surplus-value … Direct wage decrease [is] crucial to the analysis of capitalism as imperialism and a world system. (Higginbottom 2011, p. 284)

---

workers' physical capacity, in contrast to the exploitation resulting from an increase in her/his productivity, and tends normally to express itself in the fact that labour-power is remunerated below its actual value.' (Marini 1973, p. 93; my translation)

The capitalists' monopoly impulse, i.e. the desire to capture surplus-value at the expense of other capitalists, along with their insatiable lust for super-exploitable labour, combine together to dictate capitalism's innate, inexorable imperialist trajectory, the only possible path that capitalism could have taken. *Both* elements—monopoly and super-exploitation—are absolutely essential to the concept of imperialism; to define imperialism solely in terms monopoly is one-sided and therefore false, and forgets Lenin's other, oft-repeated definition of it: 'the division of nations into oppressor and oppressed [is] the essence of imperialism' (Lenin [1915] 1964, p. 409), which today is expressed in the apartheid-like structure of the global workforce and the super-exploitation that it engenders.

If this is so, *why isn't super-exploitation at the centre of Lenin's concept of imperialism*, as expounded in *Imperialism, the Highest Stage of Capitalism* (Lenin [1916] 1964), alongside monopoly?

The short answer is that *it is* at the centre, and you will find it if you look for it, but it is furled up, and for good reason. As argued above, it is unreasonable to expect to find, in the writings of Lenin and others writing at the time of the birth of capitalism's imperialist stage, a theory of imperialism that is able to explain its fully-evolved modern form. One long century ago, the relation between imperialist and oppressed nations was largely a relation between capitalist and pre-capitalist social formations, in stark contrast to today's world, in which capitalist social relations have established almost total dominance, and relations between imperialist and oppressed nations are almost entirely within the orbit of the capital–labour relation. Lenin could not have included a conception of how value is produced in globalized production processes because the large-scale occurrence of this phenomenon pertains to a later phase of capitalist development than the one in which he was living. These circumstances have resulted in an inevitable disconnection, persisting right to this day, between

Lenin's theory of imperialism and Marxist value theory—although it was not inevitable that this disconnection would persist right to this day. For this we have ourselves to blame.

As Lenin said in the preface to the French and German edition of his famous pamphlet on imperialism (Lenin [1921] 1964, p. 193), 'enormous *superprofits*' accrue to 'a *handful* . . . of exceptionally rich and powerful states which plunder the whole world'. These superprofits *arise from imperial privilege*, from monopolistic violation of equal exchange. Imperialist superprofits can take many forms: from slavery to all other vile forms of extortion, naked thievery and lawlessness—or super-exploitation, *in which the exchange being violated is the one that takes place between capital and labour* (mediated by immediate employers, national bourgeoisies, etc.). In this case, the equality being violated is the equality between proletarians, the central importance of which was stressed at the beginning of this essay.

The capitalists' insatiable lust for super-exploitable labour, their permanent desire to reap where they have not sown, to violate the equality of exchange between free agents, provides the *impulse* for imperialism, which is why imperialism cannot be reduced to monopoly, or to the 'over-ripeness'/hypertrophy of capital, or to any other of its effects. Global labour arbitrage—the substitution of relatively highly paid workers at home with low-wage workers in subject nations, the driving force of the globalization and global shift of production that has characterized the neoliberal era—is the purest expression of this impulse.

Super-exploitation of wage labour played a minor role in the early stages of capitalist imperialism, when imperial plunder manifested itself in rapacious extraction of mineral resources, often with forced labour, along with diverse forms of financial usury and extortion. Unequal exchange, i.e. disadvantageous and deteriorating terms of trade of the South's primary commodity exports (already present, as Marini has pointed out, from the middle of the nineteenth century), attained pre-eminent importance in the long period leading to the neoliberal era; mightily contributing to exponentially mounting debt, which became a major and continuing source of plunder in its own right; finally, the globalization of production characteristic of the neoliberal era, *turned living labour into the crop to be farmed, the resource to be extracted*. And this, during the neoliberal era, *has become the predominant form of imperial plunder*.

This brings to mind a luminous idea from Evald Ilyenkov which goes light-years beyond the banalities of 'the theory of uneven and combined development' (which, for many imperialism-denying Marxists, serves as an insipid substitute for a theory of imperialism): 'Very often … the genuine objective cause of a phenomenon appears on the surface of the historical process later than its own consequence' (Ilyenkov 1960, p. 217).

CONCLUSION

Imperialism and super-exploitation are inseparably connected. The capitalists' monopoly impulse, i.e. their desire to capture surplus-value at the expense of other capitalists, along with their insatiable lust for super-exploitable labour, combine together to define capitalism's innate, inexorable imperialist trajectory. It follows that denial of the relevance and prevalence of super-exploitation is, necessarily, imperialism-denial, even if the denier continues to use 'imperialism' as a descriptive term.

REFERENCES

Amin, S. 2018. *Modern Imperialism, Monopoly Finance Capital, and Marx's Law of Value*. New York: Monthly Review Press.

Bettelheim, C. 1972. 'Some Theoretical Comments by Charles Bettelheim'. In *Unequal Exchange: A Study of the Imperialism of Trade*, edited by Arghiri Emmanuel, pp. 271–322. London: NLB.

Callinicos, A. 1992. 'Race and Class'. *International Socialism*, vol. 2, no. 55. https://www.marxists.org/history/etol/writers/callinicos/1992/xx/race-class.html, last accessed May 28, 2020.

———. 2009. *Imperialism and Global Political Economy*. Cambridge: Polity Press.

Cope, Z. 2019. *The Wealth of (Some) Nations*. London: Pluto Press.

Harris, N. 1986. 'Theories of Unequal Exchange'. *International Socialism*, vol. 2, no. 33.

Engels, F. (1847) 2010. 'The Communists and Karl Heinzen'. In *Marx and Engels. Collected Works*. Vol. 6, *Marx and Engels. 1845–48*. Digital edition: Lawrence & Wishart.

Higginbottom, A. 2009. 'The Third Form of Surplus Value Increase'. Paper presented at the Historical Materialism Conference, London. https://www.academia.edu/11418979/Third_form_of_extraction_surplus_value, last accessed May 28, 2020.

———. 2011. 'The System of Accumulation in South Africa: Theories of Imperialism and Capital'. *Économies et Sociétés*, vol. 45, no. 2, pp. 261–88.

———. 2014. 'Imperialist Rent in Practice and Theory'. *Globalizations*, vol. 11, no.1, pp. 23–33. https://www.researchgate.net/publication/263569325_'Imperialist_Rent'_in_Practice_and_Theory, last accessed May 28, 2020.

———. 2018. 'Enslaved African labour in the Americas: from primitive accumulation to manufacture with racial violence'. *Revista de Estudos e Pesquisas sobre as Américas*, vol. 12, no. 1. https://www.researchgate.net/publication/323583151_Enslaved_African_labour_in_the_Americas_from_primitive_accumulation_to_manufacture_with_racial_violence, last accessed May 28, 2020.

Ilyenkov, E. 1960. *The Dialectic of the Abstract and the Concrete in Marx's*

Capital. Moscow: Progress Publishers.

Katz, C. 2017. 'Aciertos y Problemas de la Superexplotación'. https://katz.lahaine.org/b2-img/ACIERTOSYPROBLEMASDELASUPEREXPLOTACIN.pdf, last accessed May 28, 2020.

Kidron, M. 1974. 'Black Reformism: The Theory of Unequal Exchange'. In *Capitalism and Theory*, edited by M. Kidron. London: Pluto Press.

Latimer, A. 2016. 'Superexploitation, the Race to the Bottom and the Missing International'. In *The Palgrave Encyclopedia of Imperialism and Anti-Imperialism*, edited by S.M. Bâ and Immanuel Ness, pp. 1136–50. New York: Palgrave Macmillan.

Lenin, V.I. (1902) 1978. *What Is to Be Done?*. Beijing: People's Publishing House.

———. (1915) 1964. 'The Revolutionary Proletariat and the Right of Nations to Self-Determination'. In *Collected Works*, vol. 21, pp. 407–11. Moscow: Progress Publishers.

———. (1916) 1964. *Imperialism, the Highest Stage of Capitalism*. In *Collected Works*, vol. 22, pp. 185–305. Moscow: Progress Publishers.

———. (1921) 1964. 'Preface to the French and German Editions'. In *Collected Works*, vol. 22, pp. 189–195. Moscow: Progress Publishers.

Mandel, E. 1975. *Late Capitalism*. London: NLB.

Marini, R.M. 1973. *Dialéctica de la Dependencia* [Dialectic of Dependency]. Mexico DF: Ediciones Era.

Marx, K. (1867) 2010a. *Capital, Volume I*. Vol. 35 of *Marx and Engels. Collected Works*. Digital edition: Lawrence & Wishart.

———. (1894) 2010b. *Capital, Volume III*. Vol. 37 of *Marx and Engels. Collected Works*. Digital edition: Lawrence & Wishart.

———. (1867) 2010c. *Marx and Engels. Collected Works*. Vol. 42, *Letters. 1864–68*. Digital edition: Lawrence & Wishart.

Osorio, J. 2018. 'Acerca de la superexplotación y el capitalismo dependiente' [About Super-Exploitation and Dependent Capitalism]. *Cuadernos de Economía Crítica*, vol. 4, no. 8, pp. 153–81.

———. 2019. 'Cuestiones epistémicas en el análisis de la dependencia y del capitalismo dependiente' [Epistemic Issues in the Analysis of Dependency and Dependent Capitalism]. https://herramienta.com.ar/articulo.php?id=3006, last accessed May 28, 2020.

Shaikh, A. 1980. 'The Laws of International Exchange'. In *Growth, Profits and Property: Essays in the Revival of Political Economy*, edited by Edward J. Nell, pp. 104–35. Cambridge: Cambridge University Press.

Smith, J. 2012. 'La ilusión del PIB. Valor añadido frente a valor capturado' [The Illusion of GDP. Added Value vs Captured Value]. https://contraeldiluvio.es/wp-content/uploads/2019/12/58e728_c11d10962bcd40699af02f5502da7ff2.pdf, last accessed May 28, 2020.

———. 2016. *Imperialism in the Twenty-First Century: Globalization, Super-Exploitation, and Capitalism's Final Crisis*. New York: Monthly Review Press.

Sweezy, P.M. 1981. *Four Lectures on Marxism*. New York: Monthly Review Press.

Vasudevan, R. 2019. 'The Global Class War'. *Catalyst*, vol. 3, no. 1.

E. AHMET TONAK[1]

MORIBUND COMPETITIVE CAPITALISM

One day in the 1980s, my maternal grandfather was sitting in a park in suburban London. An elderly British man came up to him and wagged a finger in his face. 'Why are you here?' the man demanded. 'Why are you in my country?'

'Because we are the creditors,' responded my grandfather, who was born in India, worked all his life in colonial Kenya, and was now retired in London. 'You took all our wealth, our diamonds. Now we have come to collect.' We are here, my grandfather was saying, because you were there.

Suketu Mehta, *This Land Is Our Land*

INTRODUCTION

In this age of globalization, the concept of imperialism has lost some of its theoretical prestige; even a passing reference is now liable to be considered banal and unsophisticated. Interestingly, the relatively recent popularity of the concept and the formulation of competing new theories of imperialism mostly focus on its *political manifestations* (such as wars and military invasions) or on the *economic consequences* of *capitalistically imperialistic*[2]

[1] Without implicating them, I am very much indebted to I.C. Schick, Vijay Prashad, and Z.Ü. Kutlu for their suggestions.

[2] I use the term *capitalistically imperialistic* to distinguish my focus from other imperialistic relations that have historically existed between strong and weak countries (territories, communities, etc.) in pre-capitalist modes

relations (such as inequality and poverty). Without denying the political significance and urgency of developing analyses of the political dominance of the advanced capitalist countries (the global North) over the less advanced ones (the Global South), I focus here on the role played by *uneven economic relations* between North and South in constituting the basis of political domination. At the same time, I see the *sources* of domestic and international unevenness as built-in characteristics of capitalist development for which the profit motive is fundamental. It is within this framework that the *mechanisms of value transfer* must be viewed as the means of reproducing unevenness among capitalist economies sustained by the global processes of capital accumulation.

Certain active participants in the current debates on new imperialism, notably David Harvey, have argued that the classical interpretation of imperialism no longer has much explanatory power, and that the direction of value transfer has been reversed in recent years.[3] While classical interpretations of imperialism—for example, those of Bukharin, Luxemburg, and Lenin—are not without flaws, I cannot agree with Harvey's dismissal of earlier contributions. Moreover, I find Harvey's speculation as to the reversal of the direction of value transfer to be unsound both theoretically and empirically. Against such views, I would argue that imperialism is alive and well and, more importantly, that it

of production.

3 As frequently cited, Harvey writes that '[t]hose of us who think the old categories of imperialism do not work too well in these times do not deny at all the complex flows of value that expand the accumulation of wealth and power in one part of the world at the expense of another. We simply think the flows are more complicated and constantly changing direction. The historical draining of wealth from East to West for more than two centuries, for example, has largely been reversed over the last thirty years' (Harvey 2017, p. 169). John Smith identifies these writers, using a rather loaded term, as 'imperialism deniers', and those who have different formulations of the mechanisms of value transfer as 'Euro-Marxists', another politically charged adjective (Smith 2016, 2018).

constrains attempts at autonomous economic development in the South. Without denying the empirical difficulty of estimating its *full* and *net* amount, there is no doubt that imperialist countries continue to extract wealth from the Global South.

It is also worth noting that most of the newer conceptualizations of imperialism since Lenin (and even since Hilferding and Hobson) have been based on the idea of power, specifically the power of large, *monopolistic* firms. Lenin's claim was straightforward enough: capitalism had finally arrived at its *final stage*—monopoly capitalism—which was imperialism. I should add that a number of conceptual modifications to the concept of monopoly capitalism have been proposed since Lenin's sketchy formulation of the last stage of capitalism. In particular, the reconceptualization due to Paul Baran and Paul Sweezy, which took monopoly to be the absence of competition and argued for the inapplicability of Marx's theory of value, have dominated most analyses of modern capitalism on the Left.

But is that really so? And how exactly did competition disappear during the late nineteenth century? I would argue, on the contrary, that competition intensified rather than disappeared as capitalism developed and went through the process of centralization and concentration of capital. Those who have claimed that the current stage of capitalism should be understood as *monopolistic* have relied primarily on the implied notion of *free competition* (or *pure* or *perfect competition*) vis-à-vis the earlier phase of capitalism,[4] a notion that bears no relation to Marx's

4 Interestingly enough, various aspects of real capitalist competition, as initially formulated by Marx, are attributed to monopoly. To demonstrate the needless use of monopoly and the meaning and functional applicability of competition to modern capitalism, I replaced the term 'monopoly' by 'competition' (with minor modifications) in the following quote from Smith's new book on imperialism. As readers will attest, the modified quote makes perfect sense and the need for the term 'monopoly' is, to say the least, questionable: '*Competition* comes in many forms. Some pertain

conception of real competition as war among units of capital (and among the workers themselves).[5] Marx assumed that this war-like competition operates in and through nations, in other words, that it is a central regulating process functioning both domestically and *internationally*.[6] Obviously, the very basis of this competition is the fact that capital is chiefly—indeed exclusively—driven by *profit*, and that this concern not only produces cycles and crises but also *increases the reserve army of labour on a world scale.*

Although the exact opposite is generally assumed, I would argue that the role of the State has become more rather than

to production, i.e. technological innovations that allow an individual capitalist to produce a given commodity more efficiently than others; others to distribution (branding or other forms of *competition* in the marketplace, barriers to new entrants, state capture, privileged access to cheap inputs, etc.); all may be short-lived or long-lasting. Common to all forms of *competition* is that they redistribute surplus-value between capitals, enabling individual capitalists or groups of capitalists to reap extra profits by selling commodities for more than values (i.e. more than direct prices which are proportional to the values of commodities) at the expense of lower profits for the rest.' (Smith 2018)

5 Marx's notion of competition as war is one of the fundamental concepts of Shaikh's recent book *Capitalism*, where he named it *real competition*, '… antagonistic by nature and turbulent in operation. It is the central regulating mechanism of capitalism and is as different from so-called *perfect competition* as war is from ballet. Competition within an industry compels individual producers to set prices that keep them in the game, just as it forces them to lower costs so that they can cut prices to compete effectively. Costs can be lowered by cutting wages and increasing the length or intensity of the working day, or at least by reducing wage growth relative to that of productivity. But these must contend with the reaction of labour, which is why technical change becomes the central means over the long run. In this context, individual *capitals make their decisions based on judgments about an intrinsically indeterminate future*. Competition pits seller against seller, seller against buyer, buyer against buyer, capital against capital, capital against labour, and *labour against labour*. *Bellum omnium contra omnes*' (Shaikh 2016, p. 14; my emphasis).

6 It is an often-cited fact that Marx planned but was never able to complete a specific volume of *Capital*, the sixth, entirely devoted to the world economy ('the world market and crises' in Marx's words). (Mandel 1976)

less significant as capitalism has expanded globally. The primary function of the capitalist State has always been to create fertile ground for profit-making, both domestically and internationally. The fulfilment of this function goes hand in hand with an ideological framework in which the concepts of *freedom* (read: mobility of capital) and *competition* are not only central but used fetishistically. As David Gordon put it, 'the razor's edge of capitalist competition has sharpened: local enterprises are increasingly constrained to match the lowest-cost producers in competitive global markets or risk getting their wrists slashed' (Gordon 1998, p. 28). Nowadays, it is said, every country must submit to the dictates of world competition. Without 'world-class' products, so the thesis goes, the standard of living of one's own country is likely to stagnate, if not decline catastrophically.

In what follows, I first briefly review the main forms of value transfer from the South, noting that their relative significance has changed over the last several decades. I then focus on Marx's concept of 'rate of surplus-value' and show how it may be used empirically. In that context, I shall take the opportunity to comment on the use and misuse of the term *super-exploitation*. Finally, I suggest some of the less explored areas of research needed to improve our understanding of the nature of imperialist relations in today's extremely integrated world economy.

FORMS OF VALUE TRANSFER

Before listing some of the most important forms of value transfer—that is, of the appropriation of wealth by the capitalists of the North from the working class of the South—it must be pointed out that the very existence of value transfer should not be interpreted as the cause of the unevenness between the regions of the world. Capital accumulation and the global expansion of capitalism have both been uneven and integrated since the beginning. The corresponding historical processes are, by their nature, largely determined by various economic and political factors. The direction and the amount of *net* value transfer between the regions are rather complicated; as they flow from the South to the North they obviously contribute to the perpetuation of imperialistic relations, if not to their creation.[7]

One of the most prominent Marxist formulations of value transfer from the South to the North is Arghiri Emmanuel's *theory of unequal exchange.* In challenging Sweezy's view that the equalization of the rate of profit on a world scale is not possible because of the immobility of capital, Emmanuel has pointed out that although one may speak of the relative immobility of labour, which produces persistent international wage differences, capital is mobile and tends to equalize profit rates across the globe. This process of equalization implies that the profit rate in the countries of the South is generally lower than that in the North because of the transfer of *profits* (*surplus-value*) due to the lower organic composition of capital in the South (Shaikh 1980, p. 298).[8] A critical presentation of Emmanuel's highly creative application of Marx's theory of value to the world economy would be beyond the scope of the present essay. I should note, however, that Emmanuel's theory of unequal exchange has been both criticized and extended by other Marxists including Javier Iguiñiz, Charles Bettelheim, Samir Amin, Ernest Mandel, Anwar Shaikh, and Nail Satlıgan.

Another form of value transfer is based on the *portfolio*

7 For a detailed discussion of these points, see Shaikh's seminal article (in two parts) on foreign trade, the law of value, and unequal exchange (1979, 1980). This article is also useful for identifying the differences among the leading theoreticians of unequal exchange like Arghiri Emmanuel, Ernest Mandel, and Samir Amin. I should indicate that some of the points in Shaikh's piece were also developed by Javier Iguiñiz (1999) in his doctoral dissertation (supervised by Shaikh) at the New School.

8 One recent empirical work on unequal exchange suggested that for the South, the transfer of value outflow ranged around 10 to 20 per cent (Ricci 2019).

investments and international indebtedness of the South. The former has to do with the repatriation of those profits obtained from speculative investment of money capital in stocks, bonds, foreign exchange, and a variety of other financial instruments; the latter is based on the gains of exorbitant interest payments imposed on the debtor countries of the South.

Historically, one of the principal forms of value transfer has been the repatriation of profits based on direct investment by the capitalists of the North in the countries of the South. Since Lenin's pamphlet on imperialism, foreign direct investment (FDI) has been considered a leading characteristic of modern capitalist imperialism. As capitalism developed, the primacy of *commodity capital* (both in appropriating natural resources and raw materials from the South, and in selling finished commodities there) has been replaced by *productive capital* (foreign direct investment).[9] Given its historical significance, the centrality of this form of value transfer and the overemphasis (by the early theorists of imperialism) of FDI are understandable. However, a couple of observations must be made given recent patterns of FDI inflows. The first point has to do with the fact that FDI inflows to developed economies have lately been larger than those to developing economies (44 per cent in 2018, excluding China). In the current era of globalization, FDI inflows to developing economies exceeded those to developed economies for the first time in 2018 (54 per cent, including China) (UNCTAD 2019). However, this first-ever phenomenon is an *anomaly* according to UNCTAD:

> FDI flows to developed economies reached the lowest point since 2004, declining by 27 per cent. Inflows to Europe halved to less than $200 billion, due to negative inflows in a few

9 A highly original and early conceptualization of the transition from the domination of one type of capital circuit to the other has been proposed by French Marxist Christian Palloix (1977).

Figure 1: Developing Economies FDI Share With and Without China.

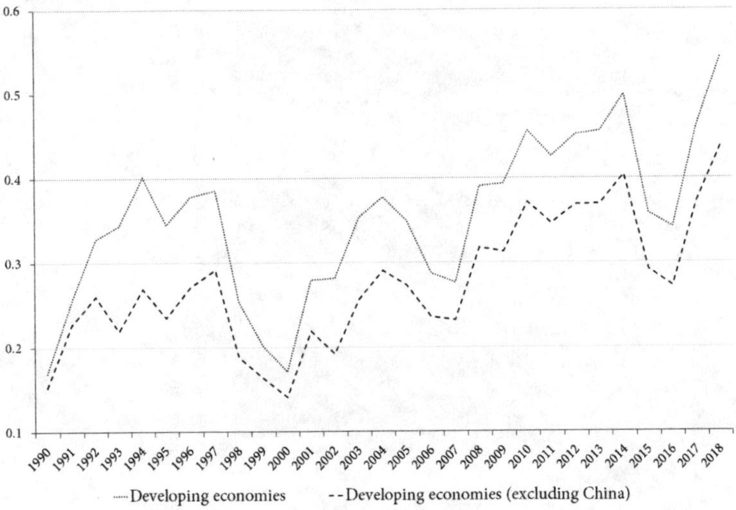

Source: Based on data in UNCTAD (2019).

large host countries as a result of funds repatriations and to a sizeable drop in the United Kingdom. Inflows in the United States also declined, by 9 per cent to $252 billion. Flows to developing countries remained stable, rising by 2 per cent. As a result of the increase and the anomalous fall in FDI in developed countries, the share of developing countries in global FDI increased to 54 per cent, a record. (Ibid.)

Secondly, and contrary to the generally held assumption on the Left, foreign capital does not flow to the South because wages there are *mostly* low. This has been persuasively argued by David Gordon, who found that the importance of the factors of *low wages and surplus-labour abroad have been much exaggerated*, and that there are other factors influencing capital's decision to invest in other countries. Gordon identified three factors as most important: *proximity to large home markets*; *relatively stable price and trade horizons*; and *the general institutional climate and its prospective*

Figure 2: Leading Factors for Foreign Direct Investment.

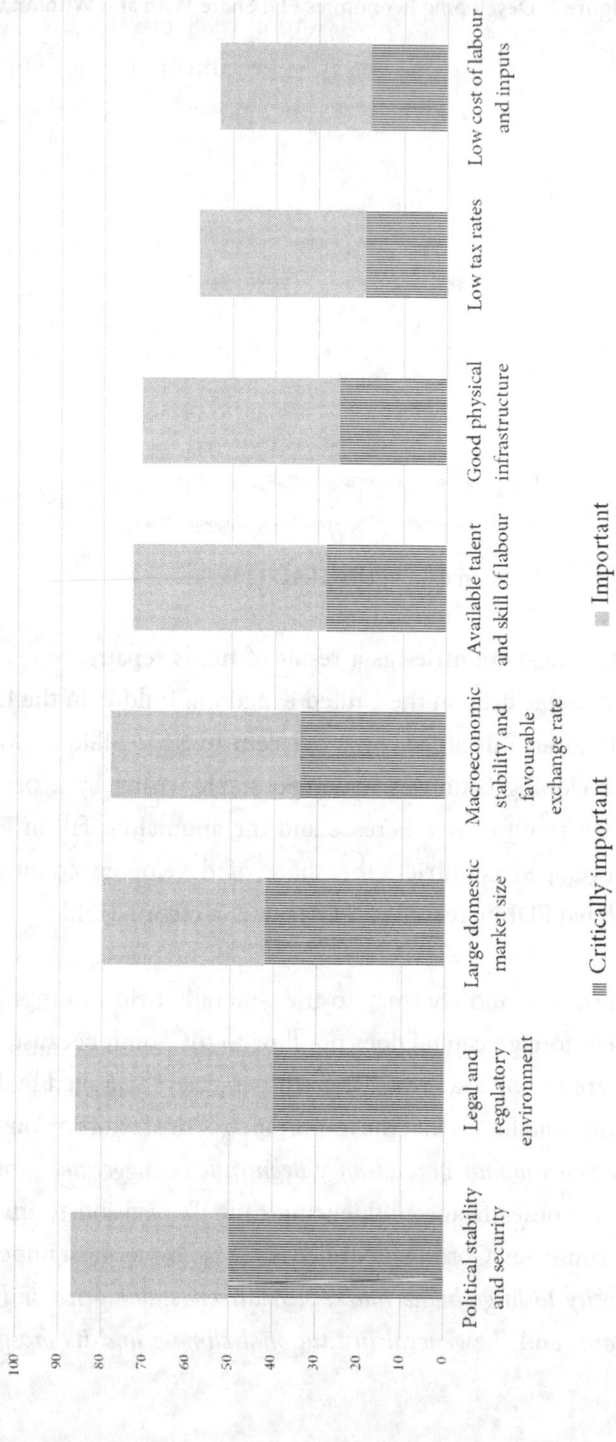

Sources: Based on data in World Bank (2018).

evolution over a decade's time (Gordon 1988, p. 59).

As recently as 2017, when 754 executives of major multinational corporations were surveyed about the factors relevant to their decisions on investing in foreign countries, the factor of low wages was not cited among the most important (World Bank 2018). In fact, among those factors considered 'critically important' or 'important' for investment decisions were *political stability and security, legal and regulatory environment, large domestic market size, macroeconomic stability and favourable exchange rate, available talent and skill of labour, good physical infrastructure*, and *low tax rates*, with respectively 87, 86, 80, 78, 73, 71, and 58 per cent respondent support. On the other hand, the factor of *low cost of labour and inputs* was only considered important by 53 per cent (ibid.). It is remarkable that what Gordon identified thirty-two years ago as reasons more important than low wages in decisions regarding foreign investment remain so among those shared by MNCs' decision-makers!

A final point regarding the significance of foreign profits from the viewpoint of US capital (and workers) is illustrated in the following graph (Figure 3). US-based MNCs' repatriated profits as a percentage of total US profits have fluctuated between 20 per cent and 50 per cent (if we exclude the period of the 2007–09 crisis) since 1998.

Considering the fact that only about 50 per cent of those 'foreign profits' originated from countries in the South, one should not exaggerate their contribution, which varied between 10 per cent and 25 per cent of total US profits. Relatedly, regarding the issue of whether or not the 'labour aristocracy' in the US is supported by transferred profits, I would highlight the fact that the portion of repatriated profits from the South corresponds roughly to only 6–7 per cent of total wages. This last figure calls into question the extremely unrealistic assumption that all transferred

Figure 3: Foreign Profits as Percentage of Total US-Profits and Domestic US-Wages, 1998–2018.

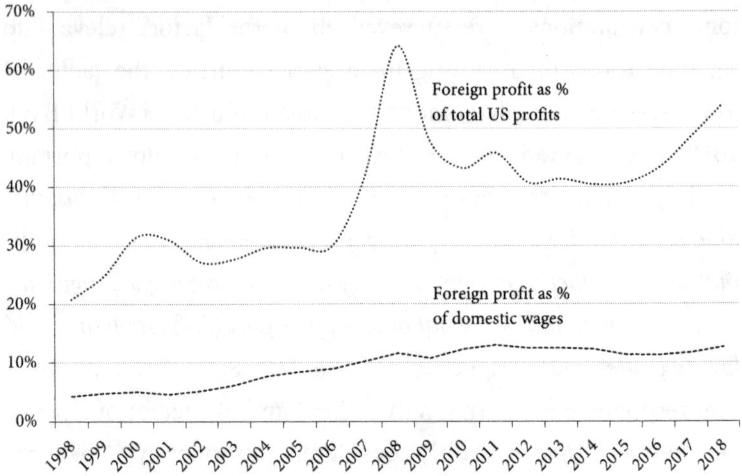

Sources: Corporate Profits from NIPA, Tables 6–16 B-D: line 2, Domestic Industries; line 6, Receipts from Rest of the World; Employee Compensation from NIA, Table 1.13: line 6, Compensation of Employees (Post 2010, p. 21)

foreign profits are fully allocated to US workers, while the US MNCs retain none (Post 2010).

THE RATE OF SURPLUS-VALUE AND IMPERIALISM

The rate of exploitation is one of the most important concepts in Marx's theory of value. It is the basis of the distribution of income—hence of the rate of profit—as well as being central to our understanding of the specific nature of capitalist society (Amsden 1981, p. 229). Moreover, it is this measurement, namely the ratio of one component of *value-added* (*surplus-value*) to the other (*variable capital*, i.e. the wages of productive workers), which allows us to show how much the worker contributes to the increase of value in the production process and how this value-added is shared between capitalists and workers. It should be noted that even if the worker is paid more, the rate of exploitation still increases by virtue of mechanization (cheapening of consumption goods) and efficient management of the production process (raising the intensity of labour). Because the rate expresses quantitatively the contradictory interests of the capitalists and the workers, there is an implied radical politics in the analysis of the rate of exploitation. It enables workers to see how much of the share of the value produced is appropriated from them by capitalists, and therefore to make the case for a different way to organize production and end exploitation (Tricontinental 2019).

The workers sell their labour-power for a set amount of money, known as *variable capital*. When they start to work on the production of commodities, it takes them a fraction of their working day to make enough commodities to cover their own wages. Marx called that the *necessary labour-time*. It was *necessary* because workers must reproduce their depleted labour-power continuously. However, the very amount of *necessary labour-time* (or the corresponding amount of wages) varies across different epochs and countries due to the fact that the consumption baskets of workers consist of different amounts of goods and services. In some countries, the standard of living is lower than in others, which means that the necessary labour-time is also shorter, holding wages down. The remainder of the working day, after the necessary labour-time has elapsed, is the *surplus labour-time*. It is the time that the worker spends producing commodities that are above and beyond the amount they need to produce in order to pay for their wage bill. Hence, the rate of surplus-value can also be expressed as a ratio between *surplus labour-time* and *necessary labour-time*. Whether in the form of the ratio of *surplus-value* (s) to *variable capital* (v) or of *surplus labour-time* to *necessary labour-time*, the rate of surplus-value is considered a quantitative expression of the *exploitation of the worker*.

What I have briefly presented above is well known to anyone familiar with the basics of Marxist economics. The less familiar terrain is the way in which the rate of surplus-value concretely expresses itself in the reality of capitalist economies, and its empirical estimation. My work with Anwar Shaikh presented a method for the estimation of the rate of surplus-value for the US economy during the period 1948–89, in step-by-step fashion (Shaikh and Tonak 1994).[10] Since this work is available for interested readers, I will simply reiterate one of its main findings: the rate of surplus-value (s/v; *the rate of exploitation of productive workers*) increased by over 40 per cent during the postwar period, from 170 per cent in 1948 to 244 per cent in 1989 (and, according to Mohun's updated estimates, to almost 300 per cent in 2001).

Both the level of the rate of surplus-value in the US and its staggering increase allow us to make some additional comments about Marx's extraordinary foresight regarding the rate's rhythm and function. Marx predicted that, as capitalism develops, the rate of surplus-value will necessarily go up—and so it did, almost twofold in fifty years in the case of the US. Again, as pointed out by Marx, capitalists resort to a variety of means to increase the rate of surplus-value, especially during periods of falling profit rates, in order to counteract the tendency of profitability to decline. It is now a well-established fact that 'the repression directed against labour beginning in the Reagan era had the clear effect of reversing the postwar pattern of profitability' (Shaikh 2016, p. 731), as manifested in the increase of the rate of surplus-value from 200 per cent in the 1980s to 300 per cent in the 2000s (Mohun 2005).

Because the difference between the rates of surplus-value

[10] This work provided the methodological basis of other similar estimates in many different countries, including those on Greece by Paitaridis and Tsoulfidis (2012), Tsoulfidis and Tsaliki (2014), and on Turkey by Karahanoğulları (2009). I should also mention the important contributions of Simon Mohun (2005) in updating our estimates (with some corrections) based on the availability of newer data sets.

in the countries of the North and those of the South has been a central issue in developing the notion of 'super-exploitation' (and, on that basis, even a theory of imperialism) it will be worthwhile to cite some estimates from the South. Let us look first at estimates of the rate of surplus-value in Turkey and Greece, and then briefly cite a few other estimates to establish a comparative basis.

Regarding estimates for Turkey, unquestionably the most comprehensive and sophisticated analysis was made by Karahanoğulları in his book *Is Marx's Value Measurable?* Karahanoğulları analysed the period 1988–2006 and documented the fact that the average value of the rate of surplus-value during that period was 239 per cent—changing from 254 per cent in 1988 to 312 per cent in 2006 (Karahanoğulları 2009).[11]

In another empirical work relevant to the discussion of imperialism in the context of Turkey, Tonak (1998) explored the *profit–wage ratios* (a pseudo-indicator of the rate of surplus-value) in some of the FDI-intensive enterprises during 1996. Based on data for the leading 500 companies collected by the İstanbul Chamber of Industrialists and six major joint ventures with foreign capital, the results were consistent with our theoretical expectations. Because these joint-venture firms are technologically sophisticated and able to implement managerial supervision to increase the intensity of labour, they all have much higher profit–wage ratios than the average for the 500 firms. To give a concrete sense of the extent of 'exploitation' as indicated through the profit–wage ratio, we can cite the fact that four firms (from varied sectors including tobacco—Philip Morris—and automotive—Renault) had 4–6 times higher profit–wage ratios than the average, and the other two (both car manufacturers—Toyota and Fiat—that are joint enterprises with Turkish capital) had slightly more than 3 and 2 times the average, respectively.

[11] Some of the earliest estimates were made by Tonak (1980), where the figures changed from 376 per cent in 1950 to 352 per cent in 1975.

Table 2: Comparative Rates of Surplus-Value.

	USA	Greece	Turkey	Philippines	Mexico	Puerto Rico
Shaikh and Tonak (1994)	170% (1948) 244% (1989)					
Mohun (2005)	200% (1980) 300% (2001)					
Tsoulfidis and Tsaliki (2014)		150% (1970) 200% (2006)				
Karahanoğulları (2009)			254% (1988) 312% (2006)			
Tonak (1980)			376% (1950) 352% (1975)			
Venida (2007)	100% (1947) 112% (1967)			137% (1961) 243% (1994)	217% (1970) 292% (1976)	97% (1948) 93% (1963)

Source: Compiled from various studies by the author.

Table 2 (contd.): Comparative Rates of Surplus-Value, for manufacturing, average, 1969–77.

USA	249 %
Germany	259 %
Sweden	220 %
Canada	202 %
Egypt	262 %
Turkey	388 %
India	244 %
South Korea	465 %
Bolivia	346 %
Panama	402 %
Puerto Rico	303 %
Malawi	352 %

Source: Amsden (1981).

The relatively recent work on the rate of surplus-value in Greece is by Lefteris Tsoulfidis and Persefoni Tsaliki (2014); they have found that the estimated rate of surplus-value changed from roughly 150 per cent in 1970 to about 200 per cent in 2006 (ibid.).

One of the early important contributions to the literature on the comparative analysis of the rates of surplus-value in the manufacturing industry for the period 1969–77 was made by Alice Amsden (1981). Both the originality of her analysis and its relevance to our understanding of capitalism before the current period of globalization can be seen in her introductory remark:

> An international comparison of rates of surplus value throws light on the dimensions and possibilities of surplus value creation under various historical and institutional conditions. It serves as a starting point for studying how the uneven spread of capitalism on a global scale impinges on surplus value extraction in disparate social settings. (Amsden 1981, p. 229)

The end result of Amsden's findings, even allowing for the fact that her calculations were sectoral rather than aggregate for the pre-globalization period, are rather unexpected: she has found that the rates of surplus-value in the countries of the South have substantially exceeded those of the North. Interestingly enough, the rate of surplus-value among the mid-income countries of the South tends to be higher than those in the low-income countries of the South (Amsden 1981, p. 242).

As mentioned above, the difference between the rates of surplus-value in the countries of the North and those of the South has been a central idea in developing the notion of super-exploitation and, on that basis, a theory of imperialism, since the original contribution of Ruy Mauro Marini.[12] The most recent proponents of this approach are Andy Higginbottom (2010) and John Smith (2016). In particular, Smith's award-winning book received much attention and generated substantial debate. Instead of summarizing the issues of the debate, which are available especially through the blog maintained by M. Roberts (2019), I simply want to underscore some of the points of agreement and disagreement between Smith and myself.

There is no question that the global expansion of the circuit of productive capital in the form of value chains is a relatively recent and very important phenomenon. It is an area that definitely requires more attention and needs additional work, both theoretical and empirical, using the labour theory of value. It has also been demonstrated by some empirical work (including our own at the

12 From our point of view, super-exploitationists in the last analysis belong to the underdevelopment school because, for them, the issue has been how to identify the source of the 'development of underdevelopment' within the realm of the so-called *external* causes, i.e. imperialism. However, in this perspective, the underdevelopment of the South is the product of the development of the North, and in this sense the two processes are intertwined. Moreover, the super-exploitationist approach implies an attributed passivity to the working classes in both the South and the North.

Tricontinental Institute for Social Research [Tricontinental 2019]) that those firms integral to the value chains in the South have imposed much higher rates of surplus-value on their workers than their counterparts in the North. Our recent work on the iPhone 10 estimated the rate of exploitation of the workers involved in its production as above 2,000 per cent (ibid.).

Beyond those agreements, however, the fact that value transfer between North and South (or from weaker capitalist economies to stronger ones, both domestically and internationally) has multiple sources, as indicated earlier, it is rather complicated to determine its direction and net amount, let alone singling out a particular source (e.g. higher rates of surplus-value) and attempting to build a theory of imperialism around it. The concept of super-exploitation requires a clear and empirically applicable definition. Smith has attempted to do the former in his book, defining super-exploitation as arising in the South when the rate of surplus-value is higher than the average rate of surplus-value in the North.[13] However, there is no single comparative estimate of the rates of surplus-value in the book itself, even though it claims that the very concept of super-exploitation not only serves as the basis of a new theory of imperialism but also initiates the renaissance of Marxism.

CONCLUSION

To recapitulate, the theory of imperialism does need a theory of global competition, and one can be developed on the basis of

[13] According to Smith, unequal exchange between capitalist and labourer (in the sense that workers are paid below their value of labour-power) leads to super-exploitation. Within a country, some account has to made of the 'skilling problem' in Smith, Ricardo and Marx. A paper on this subject by Shaikh and Glenn (2018), in which equal rates of exploitation even within a country imply unequal wages, can be found here: https://ideas.repec.org/p/new/wpaper/1811.html.

Marx's notion of domestic competition as presented in *Capital*. This attempt involves theories of international trade, of real exchange rate determination, and of price formation through the application of a real theory of competition between sectors and within sectors internationally.[14] Hence, imperialism itself should not be understood as an exertion of power by the monopolist firms of the North on the weaker ones of the South. Instead, imperialist relations must be seen as manifestations of the very uneven and historically-determined nature of global capitalist development. These relations do contain various forms of value transfer, which are themselves means of perpetuating already existing imperialist relations rather than causing them.

[14] Some of these areas of research were covered in our earlier book (Shaikh and Tonak 1994) but also more comprehensively in Shaikh's recent book (2016).

REFERENCES

Amin, S. 1977. *Imperialism and Unequal Development*. New York: Monthly Review Press.

Amsden, A. 1981. 'An international comparison of the rate of surplus value in manufacturing industry'. *Cambridge Journal of Economics*, vol. 5, no. 3, pp. 229–49.

Botwinick, H. 1993. *Persistent Inequalities: Wage Disparity Under Capitalist Competition*. Princeton: Princeton University Press.

Emmanuel, A. 1972. *Unequal Exchange: A Study of the Imperialism of Trade*. New York: Monthly Review Press.

Gordon, D. 1988. 'The Global Economy: New Edifice or Crumbling Foundations?'. *New Left Review*, no. 168 (March–April), pp. 24–64.

Harvey, D. 2017. 'A Commentary on *A Theory of Imperialism*'. In *A Theory of Imperialism*, by U. Patnaik and P. Patnaik, pp. 154–72. New York: Columbia University Press.

Higginbottom, A. 2010. 'Underdevelopment as super-exploitation: Marini's political-economic thought'. Paper presented at Historical Materialism: Crisis and Critique, 7th Annual Conference, November 11–14, London, UK.

———. 2014. 'Imperialist rent in Practice and Theory'. *Globalizations*, no. 111, pp. 23–33.

Iguiñiz, J.I. 1979. 'Elements Towards a More General Theory of Unequal Exchange'. Ph.D. thesis, New School for Social Research.

Karahanoğulları, Y. 2009. *Marx'ın Değeri Ölçülebilir mi?* [Is Marx's Value Measurable?]. İstanbul: Yordam Kitap.

Mandel, E. 1976. 'Introduction'. In *Capital. Volume One*. London: Penguin Books Ltd.

Mehta, S. 2019. *This Land Is Our Land: An Immigrant Manifesto*. New York: Farrar, Straous and Giraoux.

Mohun, S. 2005. 'On measuring the wealth of nations: The U.S. economy, 1964–2001'. *Cambridge Journal of Economics*, vol. 29, no. 5, pp. 799–815.

Paitaridis, D., and L. Tsoulfidis. 2012. 'The growth of unproductive activities, the rate of profit, and the phase-change of the U.S. economy'. *Review of Radical Political Economics*, vol. 44, no. 2, pp. 213–33.

Palloix, C. 1977. 'The self-expansion of capital on a world scale'. *Review of Radical Political Economics*, vol. 9, no. 2, pp. 1–28.

Post, C. 2010. 'Exploring Working-Class Consciousness: A Critique of Theory of the "Labour-Aristocracy"'. *Historical Materialism*, vol .18, no. 4, pp. 3–38.

Ricci, A. 2019. 'Unequal Exchange in the Age of Globalization'. *Review of Radical Political Economics*, vol. 51, no. 2, pp. 225–45.

Roberts, M. 2016. 'Imperialism and super exploitation'. *Michael Roberts Blog* (blog). https://thenextrecession.wordpress.com/2016/03/07/imperialism-and-super-exploitation/, last accessed May 28, 2020.

———. 2019. 'HM2—The economics of modern imperialism'. *Michael Roberts Blog* (blog). https://thenextrecession.wordpress.com/2019/11/14/hm2-the-economics-of-modern-imperialism/, last accessed May 28, 2020.

Satlıgan, N. 2014. *Emek Değer Teorileri ve Dışticaret* [Labour Value Theories and Foreign Trade]. İstanbul: Yordam Kitap.

Semmler, W. 1984. *Competition, Monopoly and Differential Profit Rates*. New York: Columbia University Press.

Shaikh, A. 1979. 'Foreign Trade and the Law of Value: Part I'. *Science & Society*, vol. 43, no. 3, pp. 281–302. http://homepage.newschool.edu/~AShaikh/lawvalue1.pdf, last accessed May 28, 2020.

———. 1980). 'Foreign Trade and the Law of Value: Part II'. *Science & Society*, vol. 44, no. 1, pp. 27–57. http://homepage.newschool.edu/~AShaikh/lawvalue2.pdf, last accessed May 28, 2020.

———. 2016. *Capitalism: Competition, Conflict, Crises*. New York: Oxford University Press.

———, and K. Glenn. 2018. 'The Classical Treatment of Skilled Labor'. Working Paper 1811, New School for Social Research, Department of Economics. https://ideas.repec.org/p/new/wpaper/1811.html, last accessed May 28, 2020.

———, and E.A. Tonak. 1994. *Measuring the Wealth of Nations: The Political Economy of National Accounts*. New York: Cambridge University Press.

Smith, J. 2016. *Imperialism in the Twenty-First Century: Globalization, Super-exploitation, and Capitalism's Final Crisis*. New York: Monthly Review Press.

———. 2018. 'Exploitation and super-exploitation'. *MR-Online*, April 14. https://mronline.org/2018/04/14/exploitation-and-super-exploitation/, last accessed May 28, 2020.

Tonak, E.A. 1980. 'Artık Değer Oranının Ölçümü ABD ve Türkiye' [Now the US and Turkey Value Ratio Measurement]. *Toplum ve Bilim*, no. 11, pp. 13–48.

Tricontinental Institute for Social Research (Tricontinental). 2019. *The Rate of Exploitation (The Case of the iPhone)*. Northampton, MA. https://www.thetricontinental.org/wp-content/uploads/2019/09/190928_Notebook-2_EN_Final_Web.pdf, last accessed May 28, 2020.

Tsoulfidis, L., and P. Tsaliki. 2014. 'Unproductive Labour, Capital Accumulation and Profitability Crisis in the Greek Economy'. *International Review of Applied Economics*, vol. 28, no. 5 (September), pp. 562–85.

UNCTAD. 2019. *World Investment Report 2019*. New York: United Nations Publications.

Venida, V. 2007. 'Marxian Categories Empirically Estimated: The Philippines, 1961–1994'. *Review of Radical Political Economics*, vol. 39, no. 1, pp. 58–79.

World Bank. 2018. *Global Investment Competitiveness Report 2017/2018: Foreign Investor Perspectives and Policy Implications*. Washington, DC: World Bank.

ATILIO A. BORÓN

NOTES ON THE CURRENT STATE OF IMPERIALISM AND ON THE NEW US NATIONAL SECURITY STRATEGY[1]

INTRODUCTION

In the following pages, I will share some comments on the current state of imperialism, its impact on war and peace in today's world and, more specifically, on the present and the future of Latin America and the Caribbean. This paper will address a set of important topics because capitalism has been linked to war and militarism since its inception. Several writings by Marx and Engels expose this relationship in their description of the wars waged inside and outside the European continent. In 1857–58, in *Grundrisse*, Karl Marx states that 'war develops earlier than peace'; thus, he intends to show 'the way in which as a result of war, and in the armies, etc., certain economic conditions, e.g. wage labour, machinery, etc., were evolved earlier than within civil society' (Marx [1857] 2010, p. 45). However, between the two friends, it was Friedrich Engels who specialized in the systematic analysis of the military. He, to whom Marx gave the nickname the 'General' due to his passion on the subject of war, wrote extensively about this topic and affords Latin Americans a key source of knowledge, which should be thoroughly studied.[2]

1 Translated by Melisa Ruffini for Abrapalabra Co-op.

2 In a letter addressed to Joseph Weydemeyer he requested books and articles regarding the army and wars, and he told him that he was set to study the

Even though this topic is truly relevant, especially on a continent such as ours, which today hosts 80 military bases belonging to the US and some others to NATO, the purpose of this presentation will not be to discuss Marx and Engels's thoughts on the subject. Neither will I analyse the abundance of theories over the revolutionary war, which arose in the middle of the First World War, as Lenin, Trotsky, Rosa Luxemburg, Kautsky, and later on Gramsci, dealt extensively with this topic. A discussion on the question of war and peace is extremely necessary due to the demands imposed by the current political juncture at which we stand, and therefore, I will merely invite readers to explore the military writings by the founding fathers and the main figures of classical Marxism. In any case, suffice it to say that to the extent to which the Marxist tradition is placed at the core of the historic dynamics of a social struggle, it was obvious that the sociological and economic analysis ended up referring, in one way or another, to the social war, either openly or secretly waged. That is why in the well-known *Manifesto of the Communist Party*, Marx and Engels talk about 'a more or less covered civil war', which was being waged in bourgeois societies and the constant reference to the writings on war by Carl von Clausewitz, the most important war theorist at the time.[3]

Having provided this context, we will now touch on the main issue of this work: imperialism.

topic deeply due to the 'immense importance which must attach to the [military aspect] in the next movement'. Cf. Engels, 'Letter to Weydemeyer', June 19, 1851 (Engels [1851] 2010, p. 370).

3 I would like to thank Paula Klachko for making me focus on this topic as well as for her careful reading of the preliminary version of this work. From that same author, I very specially recommend the book written together with Katu Arkonada: *Desde abajo, desde arriba* (Klachko and Arkonada 2016), in the press in Cuba, Mexico, and Basque Country.

I. CHARACTERIZATION OF THE CURRENT PHASE OF CAPITALISM: THE THIRD WAVE OF IMPERIALIST EXPANSION

The globalization of the capitalist form of production constitutes a structural feature of this economic system. It gathers great momentum after the Second Industrial Revolution, which, by the mid-nineteenth century radically modified the transport and communication landscapes. The revolution in rail and sea transport, as well as in wireless telegraphy, provided the structural framework for global commerce and the territorial expansion of capitalism. Over a century later, in the current world, telecommunications, the Internet and the advances in air, maritime and land transport would produce identical results, but on a greater scale and with more considerable depth.

Today, we are immersed in what we can accurately call 'the third wave' of imperialist expansion. The first wave emerged as a necessary result of the Second Industrial Revolution and caused the greatest European colonial powers to divide up the world—an act of authentic looting—and was legalized at the Berlin Conference of 1884–85. Even though this global division had at its core the carving up of Africa, it also had effects on many other countries, which would later be called Third World countries. Many towns still suffer the consequences of this criminal and irresponsible division. The social tragedies, which play out today in many African and West Asian countries, can be traced back to the Berlin Conference. This first wave of imperialist expansion ends with the mass killing during the First World War and the fall of four empires: the Russian, German, Austro-Hungarian Empires, and, in slow motion, the Ottoman Empire. This wave is concluded with the triumph of the Russian Revolution, thus opening a new stage in history.

Nevertheless, what follows is an armistice rather than peace.

Some authors, such as Immanuel Wallerstein, view the First and Second World Wars as one world war, separated only with a truce of two decades in the middle, until the forces and alliances are realigned and the definitive battle, which is normally known as the Second World War, is fought. Even though the first world war meant the fall of four empires, the second saw the sinking of the two empires that were still afloat: the British and the French, with the imperial, marginal adventures of the Portuguese, the Belgians and the Dutch surviving precariously. However, the Second World War was also witness to an amazing event: the survival of the Russian Revolution and its unbelievable growth. This despite the horrors of their civil war and the invasion of several armies of the 'Western democracies' intent on killing the Soviet disease in its crib; and culminating in the Soviet Union's extraordinary participation in defeating Nazism. As a result of the Soviet Union's contribution to the defeat of the Axis powers, the old and complex structure of an international system based on the volatile agreements between the main European powers, whose reactionary axis was the United Kingdom, gave way to a more simplified, bipolar relationship: two superpowers—the United States and the Soviet Union—and their allies.

The second phase of imperialism

The redistribution of international economic, political and military power together with the massive destruction of human lives caused by this conflagration could leave nothing but marks of trauma in the consciousness of the time, especially if we take into account the fact that it was within this framework that the two greatest terrorist attacks in history took place: the atomic bombing of the helpless cities of Hiroshima and Nagasaki. It is commonly said that the second post-war period gave way to the most radiant chapter in the history of capitalism, the quarter century famously called the 'Golden Age'—between 1948 and 1973. It was during that short period, according to the Marxist theorist Ellen Meiksins Wood, that capitalism provided the best it could possibly ever offer. With the adoption of Keynesian economic theory, this phase gave way to the expansion of citizenship and social and labour rights; the creation of democratic regimes; and the strengthening of popular organizations, unions, communist and socialist parties. However, this period came to an end during the mid-seventies with the rise of neoconservatism in the developed countries, with Margaret Thatcher and Ronald Reagan leading the trend, and the establishment of bloody military dictatorships in almost all of Latin America. As Meiksins Wood clearly stated, that spring was not going to be repeated ever again. With the breakup of the Soviet Union, capitalism returned to normal and the old popular conquests were either eliminated or severely limited as the bourgeois democracies started to suffer a perverse metamorphosis that ended up turning them into shameful plutocracies, as they are today. In Europe, popular sovereignty no longer comes from the people, but rather lies in the tentacles of the Troika (European Commission, European Central Bank, and the International Monetary Fund), which removes and imposes governments at will. There are several cases that illustrate this, Greece being an egregious example. However, it is far from being the only one. In other words, if capital's domination reluctantly admitted progress for citizens' rights and democratic organizations it was due to the threatening presence of the Soviet Union and the danger of contagion from the 'Russian virus' (i.e. 'soviet communism') that could shatter the bourgeois regimes of the time. However, with the disappearance of the USSR that threat disappeared. As the Catalan historian Josep Fontana reminds us in his distinguished work, there were three terrible years between the end of the Second World War and the beginning of the 'Golden Age' quarter century. The USSR had lost 27 million lives, especially young men. The German occupation shattered 1,710 cities and around 70,000 towns. Germany and Japan saw a great part of their territories destroyed by bombings. And this devastation added up to hunger, which was the consequence of the destruction of agriculture due to the drought that ruined the crops in 1946, and the unusually cold winter of 1946–47. Fontana says that '[t]o the millions of casualties caused by the war we should add another million victims of the great famines that took place from 1945 until 1947' (Fontana 2011, p. 25).

To this huge number of people we can also add those who died in Asia, especially due to the horrors of Japanese occupation, and we easily arrive at 100 million people sacrificed at the altar of capitalism's rate of profit. This slaughter was the necessary preamble to the 'golden' years of 1948 to 1973, which went hand in hand with the quick, global expansion of US imperialism, whose origins can be traced back to the theft of large parts of Mexico's territory in the mid-nineteenth century; its early expansion into Central America and the Caribbean in the aftermath of that same century; and above all, the kidnapping of the Cuban victory over Spanish colonialism in 1898. After the Second World War, with the United Kingdom and France in shambles as their colonies rebelled, and with no enemies in sight, US expansion seemed unlimited. That was the second imperialist wave, which more or less coincides with the 'golden years'. However, with the European and Japanese economic recovery, notably visible from the 1960s onwards, the imperialist landscape starts to recognize multiple flags and not just the one with the stars and stripes of the United States. US transnational companies are gradually threatened by the rapid appearance of large European and Japanese corporate conglomerates first, and then by those of other countries, especially South Korea.

The second imperialist wave ended with the abandonment of Keynesianism, the 'return to orthodoxy' as Raúl Prebisch called it, and the rise of neoliberal globalization driven by huge technological advances in IT, telecommunications and transport. All this happens within a conservative environment created by a formidable reactionary trio of Ronald Reagan, Margaret Thatcher, and Pope John Paul II. At the end of the 1980s, the Berlin Wall falls, followed by the disintegration of the Soviet Union. At that moment, it appeared that the Western victory was assured and some thinkers and scholars from the US, and their Latin American epigones, concluded that the time of the 'new (North) American century' had arrived and that from now on the structure of the international system, or the so-called 'world order', would be 'unipolar'. Without missing a beat, the corporations and federal government agencies started to financially support the creation of a 'think tank' (the Project for the New American Century [PNAC]) for the purposes of drafting the blueprint for this new era which seemed so favourable for the United States. Hundreds of scholars, experts, and thinkers started to design the roadmap of such a promising journey. Bill Clinton, closely followed by his British butlers, did his part: he dismantled the last pieces of US financial regulations and created the world that Wall Street and the City of London dreamed of. It seemed as if everything was under control. The FTAA (Free Trade Area of the Americas) was nothing but the hemispheric manifestation of this global reorganization of an empire without rivals.

But, in Rubén Blades's words, 'life surprises you' and Washington was surprised. First and foremost, amid great celebration for the new 'American century', the 9/11 attacks took place. It was the first attack on US territory in nearly two centuries. We should remember that the United States had participated in the two World Wars and not one single shot was fired within its continental territory. The only exception was the Japanese attack on the Pearl Harbor naval base in Hawaii in December 1941. Suddenly, the country realized how vulnerable it was and that a large military budget did not guarantee its immunity. If, militarily speaking, the

United States stopped being unassailable; if China's vertiginous economic rise, which was not unexpected but certainly premature according to the empire's analysts (who had estimated such growth for the year 2030), continued unabated; if Russia could return to the forefront of global politics; if India continued its new, growing interference in international affairs; and if the consolidation of a series of regional powers such as Brazil, South Africa, Indonesia, South Korea, and Turkey persisted, then this new global landscape would be much more challenging than the one of the bipolar era. What is more, with the advances in information technology since the disintegration of the Soviet Union, given the danger posed by non-state actors, nuclear non-proliferation turned into a chimera and US 'National Security' proved even more uncertain than before.

Imperial relaunching

Combining commercial and financial liberalization with violent implementation of neoliberal policies almost everywhere, the third cycle of imperial expansion began gaining momentum during the decade of the 1990s and continues today.[4] This third cycle also impacts specific regions and countries: Russia, Eastern European countries, China, Vietnam, now treated as if they were hunting grounds for the imperialists. We now observe a reloaded imperialism that is stimulated by these new lands upon which their ambitions can be realized. There are several distinct features of these times, but I would like to focus on two. First, the increased concentration of wealth in every country, from China to the United States, with no outstanding exception at the world level. This has been recently condemned by Oxfam in their report submitted to the Davos World Economic Forum stating that according to official estimates to date, the wealthiest one per cent of the world's

[4] Paper finished before the outbreak of the Covid-19 pandemic. That cycle of imperial expansion is now over.

population controls 51 per cent of the earth's wealth, which means that it is more than what the remaining 99 per cent of world's population possesses. In line with this data, a study sponsored by Zurich University has shown that 147 huge corporations control 40 per cent of the world's wealth.

The second characteristic feature of these times has been the intensification of the arms race; the emergence of several zones of extreme military tension; and the increase in the number of wars and its victims. There are now three hotspots in the international system. First hotspot: The ammunitions dump in the Middle East, which is the result of the United States and its European allies destroying entire countries (Lebanon, Iraq, Libya, and, currently, Syria) for the purpose of stealing the oil, regardless of the human cost. This triggered a series of humanitarian crises not seen since the end of the Second World War. Second hotspot: Ukraine, and Eastern Europe more generally, where the White House and the European Union, in their pursuit to contain the 'Russian bear' promoted a coup d'état in the Ukraine with the active leadership of the State Department, personified by its Deputy Secretary, Victoria Nuland, and moved NATO troops towards the Russian–Ukrainian border. This was done despite the leaders of the Western 'democracies' solemnly swearing that NATO 'would not move an inch towards the East' after the fall of the Soviet Union. Disregarding their promises, they moved several hundred kilometres towards the Russian border. Third hotspot: The South China Sea, which is rich in oil and is disputed by several countries—China, Japan, and Vietnam among the most integrally involved. This is a situation that can easily get out of control, equal to the already mentioned ones, but especially serious. Washington can react mildly to an invasion of Russia into the Ukraine or a retaliation from Moscow against Ankara due to the shooting down of a Russian combat aircraft. But it can only react with all its strength if China, with the second largest military budget on earth, decides to attack Japan, a reliable partner and loyal vassal of the White House.

In summary, this wave, the third one in the history of imperialism, as with the other two waves, requires war as its natural consequence. This horrific reality shows, once again, the errors of the theory of super-imperialism or ultra-imperialism, developed first by Karl Kautsky and subscribed to by many of his contemporary followers. They insist on rejecting the thesis that imperialism could today—not necessarily in the past, but today—lead to a war between capitalist powers. Despite its glorious Soviet past, Russia is a world capitalist power and so is China, with its peculiarities. As stated in recent documents issued by the Pentagon and the Security Council of the United States, Russia is explicitly not labelled as a competitor, but as an enemy that must be defeated. Apart from that, we have to bear in mind that even during the bipolar era—before the dissolution of the Soviet Union—wars spread constantly on the outskirts of the global system; and the current landscape, far from being better, has gotten worse.

II. WHAT ARE THE DECISIVE FACTORS FOR THE PRESENT RETURN OF THE EXPANSIVE DRIVE OF IMPERIALISM?

How can we understand the current delicate situation? Briefly put, and at the risk of oversimplifying this presentation, we can say that there are three features of the current world order that can offer some clues to explain the warlike escalation.

Firstly, the instability of the global geopolitical balance is a key element generating tension and conflicts that upset the international system. One after the other, the diverse documents drafted by military and intelligence agencies of the United States insist on the fact that the new global landscape is full of threats to US national security and, as a consequence, the country has to be prepared for several decades of war. This is not intended to expand the global strength of the United States, but rather to keep their relative position in the global geopolitical chessboard. Peace, or the quest for peace, is barely mentioned in these documents. The basic assumption is the indefinite continuation of war, either of a 'preventive' type, as George W. Bush posited, or of a 'retaliatory' type following an attack on the United States and its citizens or its allied countries and citizens. The current multipolarism of the international system is relatively new. In the past, there was something similar, called the 'Concert of Nations', but it was an exclusively European system; neither the United States nor Japan, not even China, took part in those agreements which lasted from the Treaty of Westphalia (1648) until its spectacular collapse in the First World War. During almost three centuries, no non-European country was represented at the negotiation table. Today, it works in a very different manner because the non-European powers have reduced the influence of the declining and decadent Europe. Unlike in the past when the members of the alliance came from nations of similar culture and interests, today it is much more difficult to reach a consensus between nations with different, and in many senses contradictory, histories, political traditions and perspectives. Of course, they also have conflicting interests and, to some extent, these interests are irreconcilable. Under these conditions, attaining peace must overcome several obstacles for it to become a reality. This process highlights the Latin American exception, which is, by far, the most peaceful region in this disrupted and convulsed planet. The main Latin American leftist leaders and progressive forces have not overlooked this uniqueness, formally ratified by the approval, in January 2014, of the 'Peace Zone', within the framework of the Second Summit of the Community of Latin

American and Caribbean States (CELAC) held in Havana.

Secondly, the US military-industrial-financial complex, and to a lesser extent, its European allies, encourage and foster wars and violence. Such dreadful machinery develops from war and for war. For them, peace represents its bankruptcy and finale, and the only positive business strategy for these mega-corporations is to stimulate conflicts and rivalries. Their rate of profit is directly linked to war and is inversely proportional to peace. The power of this 'industrial-military' complex is enormous. It was denounced by President Dwight Eisenhower in his farewell presidential address on January 17, 1961, where he described these corporations as the most serious threat to US freedom and democracy. In reality, despite his words, this complex did nothing but expand its immense power until it reached monstrous proportions. If at that time it constituted a threat, today it is the dominant force that leads US foreign policy and it accelerates the progress from a democratic republic towards a plutocratic regime.[5] It is now a form of politics that, paraphrasing Lincoln, is of the (government's) money, by the money, and for the money. And since the military expenditure of the United States is the main driver of the US economy, gluing together at its core the industrial, financial and oil sectors, the government is interested in granting all sorts of guarantees to the companies who belong to this sector. Thus, these enterprises, which have a great number of

5 We have already covered this topic and we are now ratifying, making specific reference to the following: Tom Engelhardt, 'El nuevo orden estadounidense' [The New American Order], *Rebelión*, March 26, 2015 (http://www.rebelion.org/noticia.php?id=196927, last accessed June 12, 2020).

See two classical texts on this topic: Peter Dale Scott, *The American Deep State: Wall Street, Big Oil and the Attack on US Democracy*, various editions; and Sheldon Wolin, *Democracia S.A.: La democracia dirigida y el fantasma del totalitarismo invertido* [Democracy S.A.: Directed Democracy and the Ghost of Inverted Totalitarianism], Buenos Aires: Katz Editores, 2009.

Also see Juan Bosch, *Pentagonism, A Substitute for Imperialism*, Santo Domingo: Fundación Juan Bosch, 2015.

resources, became the main and essential sources of financing the expensive political careers of representatives, senators, governors, and presidents. Consequently, these so-called representatives of the people sold out any pretence of democracy in the United States and opened the doors to the constitution of the plutocracy, which today runs the country. Hence, it is no surprise to learn that from the start of the Korean War to the present, the United States has not known one single year without troops deployed and fighting abroad. It is also not surprising that regardless of the optimistic official announcements, military expenditures increased annually even after the demise of the superpower which, during the long years of the Cold War, was its main enemy—the Soviet Union. In that sense, the empire's propaganda machine proclaiming the alleged 'peace dividends' as a source of funds to help 'democratic' development of the Third World countries was nakedly exposed. The allocation of resources was not increased to facilitate the economic and social progress of the periphery countries nor was the increase in military expenditures reduced. According to the most rigorous estimations, the total amount of military expenditure in the United States surpassed the threshold considered, until recently, absolutely impossible to surpass—one trillion dollars, which amounts to approximately half of the global military expenditure.[6] With less participating companies than in the United States, the military-industrial-financial complex also operates in European countries, Japan, and South Korea. In other words, the quest for capitalist accumulation was always marked by violence. Otherwise, how could we possibly explain the 'Conquest of the West' in the US or the massive plunder of peasants in the countries of metropolitan capitalism in Europe, or the one that is constantly occurring in the periphery? In recent times, this

6 We developed such estimation in our book *América Latina en la geopolítica del imperialism* (Borón 2012).

violence has been institutionalized and deepened *pari passu*. The phenomenal growth of the military apparatus propels wars while it undermines the fundamentals of democracy, both in the developed world and in the periphery of the system.

A third ingredient that fuels war is what authors like Michael Klare have called 'the hunting for natural resources' (Klare 2012). In a world increasingly threatened by the depletion of certain strategic natural resources including water, oil, biodiversity, strategic minerals, food, and an unstoppable growth of the world's population, which towards the middle of this century will cross the ten-billion-inhabitants mark, the imperialist powers have launched a globally destructive campaign in order to guarantee access to the necessary resources needed for capitalist production, driven by the irrational and irresponsible use of natural resources. It is no mystery that the vigorous expansion of China among the Third World countries is aimed, in particular, at ensuring the supply of certain natural resources that are essential for its economy. This phenomenon is especially seen in Africa and, to a lesser extent, in Latin America. It is not necessary to be a radical pessimist in order to recognize that more often than not, what starts out as a commercial war ends up being a war in the more comprehensive sense of the term. Only one piece of data, out of many, will be sufficient to expose the inordinate use of natural resources for China's capitalist modernization. A report published in 2014 by the American business magazine, *Forbes*, shows that between the years 2011 and 2013, China consumed 46 per cent more cement than did the United States throughout the entire twentieth century.[7]

[7] 'China Used More Concrete In 3 Years Than The U.S. Used In The Entire 20th Century', *Forbes*, December 5, 2014 (http://www.forbes.com/sites/niallmccarthy/2014/12/05/china-used-more-concrete-in-3-years-than-the-u-s-used-in-the-entire-20th-century-infographic/#639f7cbc7194, last accessed June 12, 2020).

Leaving aside the specific case of the Asian giant, a good perspective on the seriousness of 'the hunting for natural resources' is provided by the Global Footprint Network.[8] Their data indicates that at this pace of consumption, the United States, the United Kingdom and France will need three to five and one-half planets to keep up with their current consumption level. This data gives us all we need to know about the Earth's sustainability. It is also useful to show the unsustainability of the 'Western' consumption pattern, very much promoted by the media and capitalist governments all around the world. Such insatiable consumption can only work if a significant part of the world population is condemned to abject poverty. There is simply not enough iron, cement, oil, and phosphate for everybody. There is not enough *water* for everybody! This is why imperialism has become more and more aggressive and bloody, ignited by the pressure to preserve the 'American way of life' to which only a minor portion of the world's population can ever have access. One last example is paper, which is produced out of cellulose, which is extracted from trees. Part of the deforestation suffered by the planet has its origin in the increase of paper consumption during the last few years. But not everybody consumes the same amount. The consumption per person per year in the United States amounts to 270 kilograms and, in Western Europe, 230. However, in Indonesia and Brazil, it amounts to 35 kilograms per person per year and only to 5 kilograms per person per year in India and Sub-Saharan Africa![9]

8 See https://www.footprintnetwork.org/our-work/countries/.

9 Paper consumption is important, for one thing, as an indicator of the hygiene of food and pharmaceutical products that are sold in the market. The inverse correlation that exists between child mortality and morbidity rates and paper consumption in the poorest countries on earth is not a mere coincidence. We looked into these matters in our book *América Latina en la geopolítica del imperialism* (Borón 2014).

III. THE NEW STRATEGY OF NATIONAL SECURITY IN THE UNITED STATES IN ORDER TO FACE CONTEMPORARY CHALLENGES[10]

In February 2015, the White House made public its new version of its *National Security Strategy* (hereinafter *NSS*). This document is the second document of its type drafted during Obama's administration. The previous one had been produced shortly after he took office and was made public in May 2010. A long period of time elapsed between the first and second documents and the international scene also underwent a dramatic change. Let's analyse some aspects of the most recent US national security strategy that are particularly relevant for Latin America and the Caribbean.

The backdrop of the document is the explicit acknowledgement, previously denied, of the rapid transition of the international system towards multipolarism or polycentrism. This already existed when the previous version of the doctrine was published. However, five years later, the features of the new emerging order acquired more definition and the acquiescent attitude of the previous document was no longer sustainable. China is not just a great economic power but has become the second largest economy on earth, or the first if we measure its GDP by purchasing power parity, and the main industrial locomotive in the world. Russia has recovered its international weight and India is undergoing formidable economic and technological progress. On the other hand, BRICS was reinstated as a power constellation whose presence could no longer be underestimated, let alone avoided. In Latin America both UNASUR and CELAC are bothersome

10 In this section, we analyse and update some of the reflections from a document submitted to the IInd International Conference 'With All and for the Good of All', held by the Oficina de Estudios Martianos ['Office of Marti Studies] of Cuba from January 25 to 28, 2016.

realities for the empire, which explains its efforts, and those of its allies such as Mauricio Macri and others, to weaken or destroy them. All of those changes speak of the depth of the hegemonic transition process[11] and the irreversible character of the decline of the imperial power of the United States. A hegemonic transition, we must clarify, does not entail that there will be another power like China or Russia which will occupy the throne left vacant by the United States, because such a throne no longer exists. With the move from the unipolarism of the 1990s to the multipolarism of the second decade of the twenty-first century, the position of the omnipotent hegemon has disappeared. In its place, there is a constellation of great powers with rather reciprocal veto capacity and none of them can unilaterally impose its will in all areas of international life. The United States is now the '*primus inter pares*' and is no longer the omnipotent nation of the past. It is the main military power, but its armies cannot win wars. They can destroy entire countries, but they cannot occupy them, 'normalize' the occupation, and put them to work for their own benefit. It first occurred in Vietnam, where the US suffered a humiliating defeat; and then in Iraq from where Washington withdrew its troops leaving a hostile government in office; and the same is happening in Afghanistan and Libya. And the same has happened in Syria.

Of course, the United States is still the most powerful country in the world. However, its relative power is not the same as it was before. It is no longer the power it was during the 1990s when, while the Soviet Union disintegrated, its degree of freedom was virtually limitless. Today, it stumbles about in the economic, political and cultural arenas. This new reality underlies the pessimistic reflection of the main strategist of the empire, Zbigniew Brzezinski, when he

11 Here 'hegemonic transition process' refers to the above mentioned transition from American unipolarism to multipolarism, or the development of the crisis of US imperialism and the re-emergence of Asia as a 'new hegemon'. In the next chapter, Gabriel Merino discusses this process in detail.—*Ed.*

devotes the first chapter of his latest book to the 'declining longevity of the empires' (Brzezinski 2012).[12] The prestigious magazine *Foreign Policy* reflects on the same situation in a section called '*[US] Decline Watch*', which is a kind of observatory of the decline of the United States in numerous areas of the world economy.

In our aforementioned book, *Latin America in the Geopolitics of Imperialism*, we quoted a special report drafted by the Pentagon in which it was foreseen that in the following years and until 2030, Washington had to get ready to live in a much more hostile and competitive world. According to that document, the United States Pentagon will have to deal with five categories of international actors: friends, allies, competitors, adversaries, and enemies, all of them testing their strength in the global arena. The last two will question the presence of the United States on all fronts; but the first three will subsequently assert their interests so that they will not always unconditionally give in to North American supremacy. The conclusion is that wars are going to be a permanent condition that the United States will have to face during the next twenty or thirty years.

This is the backdrop upon which the imperialist strategists drafted the document we are analysing. The text is structured around four big topics: security, prosperity, values and international order. And the starting point of the document comes as no surprise: it is the reassertion of the essential character of the United States as a nation and as a guarantor of freedom and justice on earth. That is why it starts by saying that what is under discussion is not whether the United States will be the leader but how it will be the leader.[13] And it is in the 'how' where the greatest difficulties and

12 Some of the aspects that form the US strategic debate were initially examined within the framework of the Seminar held by the International Policy Research Center (CIPI) in Havana in the year 2013. On this matter, see the joint presentation by Atilio A. Borón and Alexia Massholder (Borón and Massholder 2014).

13 Possibly the most elaborate statement of US exceptionalism can be found,

conflicts are encountered, because the bipartisanism which existed around the US's indispensability breaks down when it comes to deciding how such global supremacy is built and maintained (*NSS* 2015, p. 2).

The document makes clear that the purpose of this strategy is threefold: 'preserve the permanent interests of the United States, its domestic security, and order as to international relations'. The document, like the ones that preceded it, does not represent the thinking of neo-colonial thinkers and politicians from Latin America and the Caribbean. They speak about the existence of a relationship of 'friendship' between their countries and the United States. Those people seem to ignore what John Quincy Adams, the sixth US president once said. He stated that 'the United States does not have permanent friends, but permanent interests'. Interests, security, and order; these are the main elements subjected to multiple and various challenges, and written about in the document being analysed.

The United States's security (and as the text puts it, that of its friends and allies) is currently being harassed by multiple threats. In a world filled with dangers, security is at stake due to: the possibility of catastrophic attacks on the territory of the United States, its critical infrastructure, its citizens within or outside the country or on the citizens of its allies; global economic crises and recession; the proliferation or use of weapons of mass destruction; epidemics of lethal diseases; climate change; disturbances in the global energy market; and the threats to security and international order that derive from the existence of 'weak or failed states', which perpetrate 'massive atrocities or favour the dissemination and strengthening of organized crime' (ibid.).

The document bears a definitively militarist tone and repeatedly insists on the need to maintain a net superiority in the

currently, in Robert Kagan, *The World America Made*, New York: Vintage Books, 2013.

field of weapons. This also applies when referring to the 'force of the economy and our values'. Nonetheless, a different nuance to the one stated in this document is provided in a speech given shortly before its publication, by President Barack Obama, at the West Point Cadets' graduation ceremony. In his speech, Obama said that even though the ultimate basis of US national security is its military strength, not all the problems and challenges posed by contemporary reality can be solved by merely resorting to military means. His words are quoted below:

> Here's my bottom line: America must always lead on the world stage. If we don't, no one else will.[14] The military that you have joined is and always will be the backbone of that leadership. But US military action cannot be the only—or even primary—component of our leadership in every instance. Just because we have the best hammer does not mean that every problem is a nail. And because the costs associated with military action are so high, you should expect every civilian leader—and especially your Commander-in-Chief—to be clear about how that awesome power should be used. (Obama 2014)

However, leadership imposes unavoidable conditions. One of them being 'the strength of our institutions' as it is called in the document. The NSS document clearly defines the example set by the United States. Nevertheless, it has become clear that challenges exist that hinder Washington in its 'divine command' of guiding

14 As can be inferred from his words, Obama continues to abide by North American messianism: the idea of the nation chosen by God to lead the fate of humanity towards a bright future of freedom, justice, human rights and democracy. And if Washington quits such mission, nobody could ever replace it. This traditional statement, in Obama, takes a less brutal form than the one expressed by George W. Bush when he publicly declared: 'God told me to end the tyranny in Iraq.' But deep inside, all of them represent the same thing.

and leading. 'Washington's political malfunction', refers to the break-up of bipartisan consensus when it comes to identifying and implementing a strategy which establishes how such world leadership must be exerted, with whom, and with what goals. This political malfunction severely discredits the US political class, both inside and outside the country, and becomes a noticeable impediment to Washington's management of their allies, partners and friends within the international system.

Five transitions

The NSS document identifies a set of five global historical transitions which have radically transformed global politics; thus, the imperatives of US security. The United States must comprehend such transitional dynamics and influence its trajectories, seize the opportunities that such changes trigger, and act with efficacy facing the risk they represent. The transitions are as follows:

First, international power and its distribution have undergone a significant change. There was a displacement of the world's economic centre of gravity with the progress of the Asia Pacific countries and, above all, China. New roles are being played by the G20, which has displaced other international organizations' institutions, such as the World Bank and the IMF. The BRICS have emerged, and they project significant influence in world affairs, especially around the edges of central capitalisms. However, as to this matter, the document specifically underscores three things: India's growth potential, together with China's, will amount to 39 per cent of the world's GDP in approximately one decade; China's rapid economic climb as the second largest economy on earth and the main driver of the world's economy; and, thirdly, Russia's aggression [sic] (*NSS* 2015, p. 4).[15]

[15] The document says verbatim: '*In particular, India's potential, China's rise, and Russia's aggression all significantly impact the future of major power relations.*' Nowhere in the document is mentioned the country or target of Russia's

This means, and the document states so in euphemistic terms, that the relative power of the United States within the international arena has decreased. It is an implied acknowledgement of what we have been observing in Latin America for a while: the slow but irreversible decline of the hegemonic power although inflexibly denied by its spokespersons even though it is obvious and it is recognized in an official document of the magnitude we are analysing.[16] This accelerates the need to study the trajectory of the decline; its impact on the rest of the world; and the aberrant ways, in terms of violence, that plague the empire during its declining phase. Exploring, in other words, whether the 'imperial landing' will be soft, rough or whether it will simply crash as a result of the harassment by the 'barbarians' that surround it.[17]

Even an author such as Joseph Nye, the traditional Harvard scholar and senior government official of successive US administrations, recognizes this mutation of international power and the weakening of the power of the United States. His language does not leave room for doubt: 'In the first half of this century, the United States will preserve its prevalence in terms of power resources, and it will keep on playing a fundamental role as to the global balance of power. … [H]owever, even though the era of the United States prevalence has not concluded, it will be subject to important changes. It is still to be seen whether those changes will increase the world's security and prosperity or not' (Nye 2004). Any new theory on 'soft power', of which Nye is one of the main representatives, is based on such a premise.

A final thought on this first transition: an explanation of how these changes are reflected in the seat of real power in the

aggression. It is more of a biased, negative and abstract characterization rather than a factual statement.

16 On the topic of imperial power decline, see Borón (2014, pp. 50–58).

17 In Washington, this tripartite vision of three possible endings moves around '*soft*', '*rough*' and '*crash-landing*', even though it is politically incorrect to speak loudly about those things.

contemporary world—the State. Many will challenge this assertion by saying that the real power in society is the big transnational company and not the State. However, in our view, this is incorrect. Companies can be small, medium or big in the same way as States. Transnational corporations have enormous influence over the State. But they do not have the monopoly for the use of legitimate power of violence required to maintain the economic and social relationships in society. This rests in the hands of the states, and this is the reason why they will, in *ultima ratio*, be the crystallization of the power relations and class domination in capitalist societies. Yet, the political scientist and diplomat Chester A. Crocker was right when he said that 'the classical image of a Leviathan State, capable of controlling, forcing, restraining, regulating, collecting taxes and recruiting citizens for their armies (and also recruiting corporations) is old' and it no longer corresponds with the reality of the State in today's world (Crocker 2015). Some states still preserve some of the classical Hobbesian attributes; but even in those cases, their abilities have been shaped by the modifications produced in contemporary capitalism. The interstices and the fractures within bourgeois society are virtually infinite. The new information and communication technologies offer many escape routes from State control, which did not exist in the past, even though they also contribute to the surveillance and control capacity of the authorities. Aldous Huxley's 'Big Brother', in *Brave New World*, foresaw this awful reality. However, this increased State-enabled audit capacity crashes up against the fact that those same technologies offer unprecedented possibilities for circumvention from and resistance to the State for those in society who resist or wish to struggle against the system, or—as in the case of the huge transnational corporations—avoid the controls that a democratic regime could impose on their activities. In the end, Crocker's thesis that 'the world is adrift and lacks leadership' has definitely concerned the agents of the US government.

Secondly, the NSS document indicates that 'power is shifting *below* and beyond the nation-state'. Even in states with weak controls due to the absence of efficient 'checks and balances' that counter the overwhelming dynamics exerted by the Executive, there are accountability demands facing sub-state or inclusive non-state actors, anchored in an increasingly empowered civil society. The examples offered in the document suggest that the mayors in the megacities and the managers of mega-corporations have a *de facto* power that cannot be ignored by state authorities. The youth and a booming middle class, both of whom are fuelled by their familiarity with the new technologies, similarly put up important barriers to state action. Even though the *NSS* is very optimistic about these developments, this may lead to the structuring of very violent non-state actors, who create instability and serious political conflicts in weak or failed states; the risks of revolutionary ruptures of unforeseeable consequences; or the return, in some regions of the Third World, of traditional despotism, willing to preserve, at any cost, the pre-eminence of the state. Crocker also believes, for instance, that the old state monopoly of international management is over. Today, numerous and powerful non-state stakeholders make their influence felt on the global stage, assisted by new information technologies and media that have empowered individuals and organizations that used to have minimal—yes, they had some—chance of influencing the global scene. The uninterrupted 24-hour news cycle, driven by the large international media companies, has the capacity (it does not always exercise it) to rescue millions of people from their indifference and isolation. However, at the same time, these global media companies maximize the influence of the giant transnational corporations; the supranational bodies, such as the G20; global organized crime; and violent terrorist militias. The 'tax shelters' that enable the dirty businesses of government and corporations, with their visible links to organized crime, mainly drug trafficking, have also given way to the emergence of new actors that move around unfettered on the international scene. However, this is not a matter of concern to those who drafted this document. The list of such non-relevant matters of concern would be too long for the purposes of this work.

Thirdly, two other great transitions of our times are the increasing interdependence of the global economy and the rapid and profound development of information technology; something to which we have previously referred. The document's authors observe the dual character of these processes: on the one hand, the internationalization of capitalist accumulation, which is euphemistically characterized by the neutral name of 'globalization' and facilitates the cooperation across borders and free markets; and, on the other hand, the simultaneous creation of vulnerabilities in the presence of perverse plans of anti-system actors. The cyberattacks, the pandemics, transnational crime (drug trafficking, human and organ trafficking, illegal sale of weapons, etc.) express an ominous new reality as expressed in the document: the recharged capabilities of those called 'violent extremist elements', whose power to act maliciously grows exponentially based on the high level of the system's interconnectedness.

The fourth transition, due to the strong alliance between Washington and Israel, pertains to the changes occurring in the Middle East and North Africa, which have triggered an intense struggle for power and, which, according to the authors, could irreparably destabilize a fundamental region of the oil economy. It is asserted, for instance, that there is an ongoing generational struggle, triggered after the Iraq War, which was explosively demonstrated with the 2011 uprisings in the Arab world that put an end to the dictatorships in Egypt and Tunisia. Within this framework, a redefinition of the relationships between the different ethnic communities and between the young citizens of the Arab world and their governments is progressing. The dangers of destabilization can have a ripple effect due to religious extremism or the rejection of autocratic governments to accept democratic reforms, and could easily light up a crucial region for the global economy.

The fifth transition comprises the changes in the global energy market, closely linked to the developments in the Middle East. The document asserts that the United States is achieving oil self-sufficiency, and it accuses Russia of using its energy reserves, mainly gas, to influence politics and to exert pressure on Europe.[18] For us, the most important issue within this document is mentioned only casually: that in the next few years the underdeveloped countries will consume more energy than the developed ones; thus altering energy trade flows and destabilizing traditional agreements.

The new international agenda

As we have already explained, there is a foreign policy agenda that has little to do with the previous 'traditional' one. Given the changes in the global landscape, it is clear that the challenges and issues in international relations are no longer the same. The agenda during the Cold War had, at its core, a set of issues: the arms race;

18 The United States has been trying to achieve 'oil independence' since the first oil crisis, in 1973, with no success in its policy. To top it all, the White House decisions to shamefully support the Islamic State policy of selling crude oil at 30 dollars a barrel to economically hurt Russia, Iran, and Venezuela, have triggered a serious crisis in the companies that used to extract shale oil and that had diminished US dependency on imported crude oil. That time is now over and the companies which exploited such unconventional oil in Texas, California, and the Dakotas have ceased activities. A recent article provides overwhelming evidence on the 'oil self-sufficiency myth'; see Matt Mushalik, 'The Myth of US Self-Sufficiency in Crude Oil', *Resilience*, January 26, 2016 (http://www.resilience.org/stories/2016-01-26/the-myth-of-us-self-sufficiency-in-crude-oil#, last accessed June 12, 2020). On the use of a resource such as gas or oil as a political weapon, the United States was the champion in the field; hence, its long-time criticism of Russia for doing the same thing as Washington did has absolutely no basis.

nuclear balance; and the wars in and between *proxies*, 'influence areas', etc. In reality, those issues revolved around what used to be called the East-West conflict, a euphemism which hid what, in the most common terms, should be called the competition between capitalism and socialism. Other issues included foreign debt, structural austerity policies and financial restrictions, migration, and matters such as gender equality and the rights of sexual minorities.

The current agenda is very different. Some of the old topics remain: the case of Greece is a good example of the issues relating to financial structural restrictions and foreign debt. But there are others on which it is even more difficult to reach consensus now than before. Among them the following are distinguishable: a) international terrorism; b) crisis and destabilization in Eastern Europe (Ukraine) and the Middle East (Syria and Islamic State); c) tensions in the South China Sea; d) militarization of outer space; e) cyber wars and cyber security; f) uncontrolled migrations and refugees due to wars and climate change; g) climate change; h) internet governance; i) biodiversity and marine resources preservation; j) exploitation of Arctic resources; and k) human and organ trafficking.

Based on the information in the document, we can provide the strategic priorities for the US.

First, the need to maintain the defence of the postwar global order: its institutions and its legal framework, as acknowledged in the document, have 'served [the interests of the United States] well for 70 years' and nothing leads us to think that a change would mean a positive contribution to the global order. Hence, any reform project proposed by the United Nations and more specifically by the Security Council that so frequently proposes support to the Third World countries, must be straightforwardly rejected. The system has worked well and any change to it would make matters worse. The repeated attempts of the peripheral countries to democratize the United Nations, and above all, the despotic and unrepresentative Security Council, clash with the crystal clear defence that Washington poses of a system that, as is stated in the document, 'has served us well'.

Secondly, the document suggests that those, like Russia, who intend to break the postwar world order rules have to pay a high price. The specific economic sanctions must remain. If it is possible, they must continue to be multilateral, if not unilateral, but acting selectively. This goes hand in hand with what was recommended during Bill Clinton's administration by Madeleine Albright and by the Republican hawks in general.[19] This form of politics has been applied to several countries in recent times; especially to those the document identifies as the enemy—no longer the competitor, but the enemy—Russia.[20]

Third, the *NSS* 2015 recommends strengthening the presence of the United States in Asia Pacific, reasserting that USA 'has been and will remain a Pacific power' and intends to keep on being a power in Asia Pacific. The recent agreements with Australia that authorized the deployment of military personnel in United States bases within its territory and the constitutional reform exacted from Japan, at the request of Washington, by virtue of which Japanese troops are now authorized to get involved in military activities overseas, are clear expressions of this policy. The will to reassert US presence in the Asia Pacific falls within the broader strategy of containing or fencing in China. That is why the

19 Nonetheless, an eminent conservative as Samuel P. Huntington had objections in relation to the rationality of politics based on unilateralism. See 'The lonely superpower', *Foreign Affairs*, March–April 1999.

20 The document does not specify where and when Moscow attacked a third country. The different types of attacks (military, political, diplomatic or economic) perpetrated by the United States are 'goodwill gestures' in favour of democracy, justice, and human rights. In short, they are proposals to spread the virtuous values of the US. The attacking parties are Russia and—to a lesser extent, for the time being—China.

document says that the 'United States welcomes the rise of a stable, peaceful, and prosperous China ... while seeking ways to reduce the risk of misunderstanding or miscalculation'.[21]

Fourth, the document stresses the need to strengthen the 'permanent alliance' with Europe and underscores the essential role that NATO, a Pentagon extension, has not only in Europe and the North Atlantic, but also in the most diverse operating theatres where United States troops are located.[22] The Ukrainian issue, presented from a completely biased perspective, is used to justify the severe penalties and economic sanctions imposed on Russia till today for its supposed attack on Ukraine.

Fifth, the document stresses the need to work towards achieving stability and peace in the Middle East and North Africa. That section is overwhelmingly superficial because it merely states that to achieve those objectives the aid to Israel, the Persian Gulf, and the friendly Jordanian monarchy have to be strengthened. There is only one and one-half line about the Israeli–Palestinian conflict and the Islamic State is not mentioned at all.

In sixth place, the document advises the White House to favour an investment flow in Africa but makes no further suggestions.

Finally, the document celebrates the advances in the Americas, which translates to the fact that, for the first time in

[21] This enigmatic phrase—'miscalculations'—most likely refers to the possibility that China, which is reinforcing its military muscle, can initiate military action within the framework of the South China Sea, specially designed to attack or neutralize Japan's presence in the arena. In a completely unusual expression of Chinese diplomacy, the Chinese Communist Party organ, the *People's Daily* published, shortly after Obama's visit to Australia to sign an agreement to deploy US bases in the country that 'Australia could be trapped in a crossfire' between the United States and China.

[22] Colombia has recently been included as 'NATO extra-regional ally'. In order to get to know the scope and the characteristics of this criminal organization, see Mahdi Darius Nazemroaya, *OTAN. La globalización del terror* [NATO: Globalization of Terror], Managua: PAVSA, 2015, with a preface by the present text's author.

history, the middle class is larger than the number of poor as the region acquired growing relevance in the global energy market. The stability of the achievements seems to be challenged in the document by a diagnosis that belies the previous optimism. In fact, it states that the region's advance is stalked 'by weak institutions, high crime rates, powerful organized crime groups, an illicit drug trade, lingering economic disparity, and inadequate education and health systems' (*NSS* 2015, p. 27). The document clearly shows Washington's support for the Peace Dialogues in Havana and trusts in the idea that 'even if a few countries … remain trapped in old ideological debates', referring to Cuba and the Bolivarian countries, and even Argentina and Brazil, 'we will keep working with all governments that are interested in cooperating with us in practical ways to reinforce the principles enumerated in the Inter-American Democratic Charter'. And as to Cuba, it maintains that 'we will advance our new opening to Cuba in a way that most effectively promotes the ability of the Cuban people to determine their future freely' (ibid., p. 28).

IV. THE POSITION OCCUPIED BY LATIN AMERICA AND THE CARIBBEAN WITHIN THE WORLD'S GEOPOLITICAL SYSTEM

Taking into consideration the outlook of the US and the questions raised in the already analysed document, it is clear that war, or the threat of a war, is the backdrop against which Latin American and Caribbean relationships unfold. We should ask ourselves then, what is the role of this part of the world.

In the first place, we are the region of the world that is gifted with the most plentiful of natural resources: only 7 per cent of the world's population, yet we have between 42 and 45 per cent of the world's available fresh water. Moreover, as the planet's lungs, we own half of the world's biodiversity. We have huge oil, gas, and strategic mineral deposits and land with extraordinary conditions for the production of all kinds of food both from vegetation and livestock. These amazing resources trigger the appetite of the US empire to subordinate, at any cost, a country such as Venezuela, whose proven oil reserves are the greatest on Earth. Those reserves are greater than those of Saudi Arabia today. This is a continent that has 80 per cent of the world's lithium reserves, a fundamental energy source for the whole electronics industry and its by-products (mobile phones, all kinds of computers, common and satellite photo cameras, video cameras, hybrid cars, etc.). Those reserves are overwhelmingly concentrated in Bolivia.[23] Nanotechnology and its amazing applications have biodiversity as its foundation of which Latin America (especially South America) has the greatest volume. Do not even mention water, which is essential for a country such as the United States, whose waste of this liquid has led it to turn the formerly unruly Colorado River, capable of carving a deep canyon, into a thin stream that does not even reach the Pacific Ocean. The imperial administrators would be extremely ignorant (and they are not) to be indifferent to such an exuberant source of wealth as that offered by our region. That is why, from the beginning of its independent life, the United States considered this part of the world as their 'backyard', their comfort zone. And that is also the reason why Fidel and Che relentlessly stated that Latin America and the Caribbean were the 'strategic rearguard of the empire'.

Secondly, since the founding years of the republic, the United States's strategic military vision has always aligned with the thesis of the 'great American island', which extends from Alaska to Tierra del Fuego. Such military strategy implies that national security in

[23] Therefore, some observers have said that lithium will mean in this century what oil meant in the previous one; Bolivia must be considered the Saudi Arabia of lithium since it has the greatest proven reserves of such strategic elements.

the United States depends on Washington's capacity to prevent non-continental powers from being entrenched in any part of the American island, or allowing hostile, anti-American governments. From the mid-nineteenth century onwards, this strategy has been improved and was carried out via its successive invasions in several countries of Central America and the Caribbean, including Mexico. The 1823 'Monroe doctrine' and its Corollary, formulated by Theodore Roosevelt in 1904, openly identify the United States's hegemonic aspiration on this extensive geography which is located south of Río Bravo. As a result, Washington can reluctantly tolerate a socialist government in an African country (such as Mozambique, Zimbabwe or Angola, at a certain time), but it responds with brutality when a small 344-square-kilometre island with a population of 90,000 inhabitants, such as Grenada, 'mistakenly' chooses a radical socialist government in 1979, under Maurice Bishop's leadership. The Reagan administration's answer to Grenada's choice of government was swift and violent. In October 1983, he sent a powerful military contingent made up of almost 8,000 men (a little under 10 per cent of the invaded population) and, in just a few days, he overthrew the government and summarily executed Prime Minister Bishop and his close collaborators. The provocation that justified this crime was the building of a new airport to make it easier for tourists to access the island, which was interpreted by Washington's criminals as a perverse plan to facilitate the landing of Soviet fighter planes in the Caribbean. Nothing even remotely similar was done by the United States in any other region of the world. The invasion of such a small country without any globally significant influence as Grenada, except in Latin America and the Caribbean, exposed the strategic importance of Latin America and the Caribbean to US imperialism.[24] The real danger for America comes from

[24] In relation to the United States's interventionism in Our America, Gregorio Selser's spectacular work is unavoidable, *Cronología de las intervenciones*

the South, the Latin American underdeveloped world. It is for this reason that with some nuances, similar arguments as the ones expressed in Grenada's case regarding a supposed threat to 'homeland security' have continued to emerge until the present. Military force was previously used with Guatemala during the Árbenz administration; with Cuba from January 1, 1959, till today; followed by intervention in the Nicaraguan Revolution of 1979; and, in March 2015, President Barack Obama proved it once again when he issued an executive order establishing a 'national emergency' due to the 'unusual and extraordinary' threat to the United States's national security and foreign policy caused by Venezuela's Bolivarian administration.

From the foregoing, we can say that Washington will oppose any genuinely democratizing process taking place in our countries. Any political force that takes office and truly tries to implement popular sovereignty will be fiercely confronted by the empire. When Obama and his collaborators speak of the 'normalization' of relations with Cuba and with the other countries in the hemisphere, what they mean is to return Latin America and the Caribbean to December 31, 1958; this is to say, to the eve of the Cuban Revolution. 'To normalize' is a euphemism that masks their intention to subordinate the countries of Our America so that they can support Washington's imperial adventures, both on this side of the world and on other continents. We are well aware of the existing bonds between the US intelligence systems (not less than 16 by the last

extranjeras en América Latina [Timeline of Foreign Interventions in Latin America], Mexico, DF: Center for Interdisciplinary Research in the Sciences and Humanities/National Autonomous University of Mexico/Academic Center for the Memory of Our America. See also the most recent work by the political scientist and Cuban historian Luis Suárez Salazar, *Madre América: Un siglo de violencia y dolor (1898–1998)* [Mother America: One Century of Violence and Pain], originally published in Cuba in 2006, but soon to be published in Colombia with a prologue written by the author of this text.

count), and the military and police bodies of the empire, with their homologous organizations in Latin America and the Caribbean. United States's government agencies train our spies, soldiers and police; teach them interrogation tactics; give them weapons and, together with the weapons, the dogmatic definition of who are friends and who are foes so that they know who to shoot; and coordinate joint exercises with our navies, armies, and air forces. The US has special war schools, such as the renovated Army School of the Americas, today known by a different name but with the same purpose, and still maintains the Inter-American Defense Board that aligns our armies in accordance with the United States's military priorities and needs. This still remains in force despite the efforts of the Union of South American Nations (UNASUR), and continues to develop and coordinate a South American containment strategy of imperialist virulence. There are some valuable exceptions such as Cuba, of course, Venezuela, and, to some extent, Bolivia and Ecuador. When discussing imperialism, violence and war are so fundamental that it shouldn't require greater explanations.

On the other hand, and commensurate with the growing importance of the 'soft coup' as a substitute for the 'old military Latin American coup', Washington made an effort to meticulously temper its bonds not only with the soldiers and governments of the region, but also, by accumulating a large amount of resources (money, staff, organizations), to 'collaborate' with the '*aggiornamento*' of the Judicial and Legislative branches in our countries as well as with the modern media. Plenty of training and field trips are regularly organized by USAID, NED (National Endowment for Democracy), and other agencies of the federal government or supposedly 'independent' organizations from Washington such as private universities and foundations, to educate Latin American and Caribbean judges and lawmakers as to 'best practices' when doing their jobs. These are, simply put, political and ideological training courses aimed at instructing participants in American values and making them receptive to the United States's national interests and their transnational conglomerates. The same happens with journalists, and the results of such politics are obvious. The 'soft coups' against Mel Zelaya, Fernando Lugo, and now Dilma Rousseff, have, as their main actors, 'independent' judges, lawmakers fanaticized to an extent not seen before in the region, and the media oligarchy, all coordinated from Washington, who relentlessly slander those heads of state and manipulate the population with never-ending lies that finally create a favourable 'opinion climate' for the coup.

V. CONCLUSIONS

Our continent is the number one priority for United States's foreign policy. It is by far the most important region in the world. We have detailed this theory in previous works, and it makes no sense to dwell on this topic here.[25] Washington can lose Angola, Namibia, Nigeria, Cambodia, and Vietnam without intervention. But it will not sit idly by at the prospect of losing Grenada, Nicaragua, Cuba, Chile, and, needless to say, Brazil or Venezuela. It can make an effort to 'contain communism', as it did during the Cold War years, and develop a series of regional alliances for this containment. The political axis of the world communist revolution (acknowledged by Washington during those years) was in Europe, more specifically in Moscow. Therefore, was Europe the first *beneficiary* of the containment strategy that George Kennan formulated for President Harry S. Truman? No! It was Latin America. In a world threatened by the deadly risk of communist domination, the first region that the United States attempted to

[25] Borón 2014. See also Atilio A. Borón and Andrea Vlahusic, *El lado oscuro del imperio. La violación de los derechos humanos por Estados Unidos* [The Dark Side of the Empire. Human Rights Abuses by the United States], Buenos Aires: Ediciones Luxemburg, 2009.

protect from such an undesired result was Latin America. In 1947, the US signs the Inter-American Treaty of Reciprocal Assistance precisely for that purpose. And what about Europe? The US had to wait two more years, until April 1949, when NATO was created. With the progressive boom in Latin America, which coincided with President Lula Da Silva's announcement of the great oil fields on the Paulist waters, the White House response was to order the reactivation of the Fourth Fleet, which had been deactivated in 1950. As a well-known American aphorism says: 'first things first'. And the first thing was Latin America. If Africa falls into the hands of communism, it is a problem; if Asia falls it is even worse; if Europe falls in the hands of communism, it is a tragedy. But if Latin America falls it would be a catastrophe of incommensurable proportions. Because Asia, Africa and Europe are far away, separated by big oceans. But from Latin America, the enemies of the Empire can advance towards the United States! This was the incredible fear awakened by the Sandinista revolution, which rattled the halls of the US government in Washington. The changes in the Latin American social and political landscape since the end of the twentieth century marked an important setback in US influence in the region. The FTAA rejection constituted a harsh defeat for the empire. The consolidation of a series of progressive governments (some leftist); the heroic survival of the Cuban Revolution; and the triumph of the Chávez revolution in December 1998, clearly defined the whole period and continues to today. The victory of the Bolivarian leader was a dazzling spark that set fire to the meadow. His charisma and his spectacular capability to communicate with the masses on the continent, helped him mobilize and excite the emancipatory dreams of the peoples and nations in the area, downhearted and humiliated under centuries of colonial and neo-colonial oppression. In Venezuela, Chávez tips the first domino, which then starts a chain reaction in the whole continent. The second government would fall in Brazil with Lula in 2002; and then Kirchner in Argentina in 2003; and then Evo Morales and Tabaré Vázquez in Bolivia and Uruguay respectively in 2005; followed by Correa in Ecuador, Ortega in Nicaragua and Zelaya in Honduras in 2006. The domino effect continued with Cristina Fernández in 2007; Lugo in Paraguay in 2008; and Funes in El Salvador in 2009, clearing the way for the FMLN [Farabundo Martí National Liberation Front] Commander Salvador Sánchez Cerén to take office in his country in 2014. In 2010, José 'Pepe' Mujica would endorse the Broad Front and ascend to Uruguay's presidency, followed in 2015 by Tabaré Vázquez. Ángel Guerra, journalist and professor at Casa Lamm Cultural Center, in 2015 posed a thesis with which we agree: 'I qualify as representing a government that, to a greater or lesser extent, is independent of the United States; is fighting against implementing Washington's "consensus" guidelines; and actively pursues unity and Latin-Caribbean integration in a multipolar world.' Based on this assessment by Guerra, we could say that the following countries share those attributes: Antigua and Barbuda, Argentina, Bolivia, Brazil, Cuba, Dominica, Ecuador, El Salvador, Grenada, Nicaragua, Saint Kitts and Nevis, Saint Lucia, Saint Vincent and the Grenadines, Surinam, Uruguay, and Venezuela.[26]

In summary, it is sufficient to recognize this radical change in the Latin American socio-political landscape to understand the profound influence of the Chavist legacy and the anxiety of the imperial bourgeoisie to return to 'normal' political relations in the hemisphere. The United States's counterattack came without delay. It began with a coup d'état against Chávez in April 2002 and continued until its failure with the oil strike of December 2002

[26] See Guerra's article in his blog in *Telesur*: 'El presunto "fin del ciclo progresista"' [The Alleged 'End of the Progressive Cycle'], August 20, 2015 (http://www.telesurtv.net/bloggers/El-presunto-fin-del-ciclo-progresista-20150820-0001.html, last accessed June 12, 2020).

– February 2003. These initiatives were defeated, but not before having a boomerang effect in the hemisphere, culminating with the FTAA in 2005. The empire was undaunted and attacked once more. They attempted to produce a coup d'état and secession in Bolivia in 2008; a 'legal-parliamentary' coup against Zelaya in 2009; a frustrated coup against Correa in 2010; a successful 'legal-parliamentary' coup against Lugo in 2012; and violent protests, '*guarimbas*', in Venezuela in February 2014. Finally, they engineered a 'legal-parliamentary-media' coup against Dilma Rousseff, which ousted her from the Palácio do Planalto in September 2016.

Currently, new attacks are in the pipeline. On the one hand, the tricky 'normalization' with Cuba, necessary to appease the dissatisfaction of the region's governments with the absurd and unfair blockade, failed to remove the 'economic suffocation' of the rebel island; a diplomatic offensive and media terrorism goes on without pause against Venezuela; dirty and slandering campaigns against Evo Morales in Bolivia which finally ended up in a coup d'état in November 2019; a scandalous lawfare operation against Lula, preventing him from running for president in 2018; constant judicial harassment against Cristina Fernández and her son in Argentina. In Peru, the constant presence of the United States (we should note that according to the last survey, it is the South American country with the greatest number of US military bases deployed within its territory) and the deterioration of the democratic process in the last presidential election, reduced the political debate to the extreme right-wing and only provided the Peruvian people a 'choice' between Pedro Pablo Kuczynski and Keiko Fujimori. The White House launched a campaign promoting the Pacific Alliance, a trick played by the US to mitigate or completely neutralize China's influence in the hemisphere. It should be noted that three out of the four countries that were originally signatories to the Alliance—Mexico, Colombia, and

Peru—are suspected of using their state apparatuses to support drug trafficking and paramilitarism. Only Chile is still free from such accusations, according to US media.

Given these circumstances, or rather, taking into consideration the structural conditions that rule the relationship between the empire and its main vassals, it is easy to understand that Latin America and the Caribbean was and is a region of permanent, relentless attacks by the US, and thus, it is not by chance that this region, since the beginning of the twentieth century, is also at the global cutting edge of the resistance to imperialist extortion. Within this context, there is a country which plays a significant role in Our America: Colombia.

In this regard, the execution, in June 2013, of a cooperation agreement between Colombia and the North Atlantic Treaty Organization has caused a foreseeable concern in Our America. To justify its decision, President Santos indicated that Colombia has a right to 'think big' and that he is going to try to make his country one of the best, 'no longer of the region, but of the entire world'. He kept on saying that 'if we achieve such peace', in reference to the peace talks taking place in Cuba and with the approval of the hosts, Norway and Venezuela, 'our Army is in the best position possible to stand out at an international level. We are already standing out on several fronts'. Shortly afterwards, he did associate with NATO, an organization that has committed innumerable war crimes and massive abuses of human rights, perpetrated within Europe (we should recall the bombarding in the former Yugoslavia and the massacre in the Balkans), as well as interventions like the destruction of Lebanon, Iraq, Libya; its complicity with Israel's fascist government in its continued genocide of the Palestine people; and now its collaboration with the terrorists who attacked Syria and are sowing death and destruction in the Middle East.[27]

[27] For Santos's statements, see 'Santos solicitará el ingreso de Colombia a la OTAN' [Santos Will Request the Entrance of Colombia to NATO], *Infobae*,

Jacob David Blinder, a Brazilian writer and journalist, was one of the first to warn about the implications of the decision by the Colombian president. Until now, the only country in Latin America 'which was an extra-NATO ally' had been Argentina which acquired a disgraceful status during Carlos S. Menem's disastrous administration, and more specifically, during 1998. This administration took part in the First Gulf War (1991–92), and was compliant with Washington-imposed rules regarding several political matters, such as dismantling the missile project Condor and freezing the nuclear programme that, for decades, had unfolded in Argentina. The Left retaliated against the government with two attacks: one on the Israeli Embassy and one on American Medical Informatics Association. Such was the price that the Argentinian government paid for having associated with the North Atlantic terrorist alliance.

The status of 'extra-NATO ally' was created in 1989, not by NATO, but by the Congress of the United States, as a way to reinforce the military bonds with countries outside the North Atlantic area, which might be helpful in the numerous wars and political destabilization processes that the US deploys in the most remote corners of the Earth. Australia, Egypt, Israel, Japan, and South Korea were the first to enter, followed by Argentina and now Colombia. The purpose of the US Congress's initiative, according to Pentagon documents, was clear: their need to strengthen and legitimize endless military adventures, unavoidable during the next thirty years, with a 'multilateralism' halo that they truly did not have. This inclusion of extra-regional NATO allies, which is being fostered in the rest of the continents, reflects the demand imposed by the transformation of the US armed forces in their

---

June 1, 2013 (http://www.infobae.com/2013/06/01/1072485-santos-solicitara-el-ingreso-colombia-la-otan , last accessed June 12, 2020).

On NATO's sinister role, see the entire study by Mahdi Darius Nazemroaya, *OTAN: La globalización del terror*.

move from a prepared army to fight in limited territories, towards an imperial legion, with its different kinds of military bases (more than a thousand on the entire planet), its regular forces, its 'fast deployment' units and the growing army of 'contractors' (i.e. mercenaries) that is prepared to intervene in just a few hours in order to defend US interests in any global hotspot. With its inclusion as an 'extra-NATO ally', Colombia is at the disposal of this disgraceful imperialist army and, internally, reinforces the militarization of the country, which has witnessed civil war for over half a century, and which clamours for peace.

Even though Argentina constitutes a pathetic precedent (which in 2012, fortunately, lost the status of 'extra-NATO ally'), the Colombian case is very special, because for decades the country received, especially within the framework of Plan Colombia, very significant economic and military support from the United States—by far the biggest amount given to any country in the region. Support to Colombia was only surpassed by monies given to Israel, Egypt, Iraq, and South Korea. When Santos declared his desire to open the country to the 'entire world', this meant his desire to become a Washington accomplice to mobilize its well-equipped forces beyond Colombian territory and to intervene in countries that the empire aims to destabilize.[28] And the fact that Venezuela is on that list is no secret to anybody. Despite the announcement, however, he didn't seem too willing to send troops to Afghanistan, Syria, and other military theatres. The aspiration of the Colombian right-wing, which has been permanently in office, has been to become, especially since Álvaro Uribe Vélez's presidency, the 'Israel of Latin America', setting itself up, with NATO's support, as the regional police to surveil, threaten, and eventually attack neighbours such as Venezuela, Ecuador, and others like Bolivia,

[28] It is no secret that Colombian armed forces are the only ones in the region that have been fighting for several decades. No other army in the region has a precedent remotely similar to that one.

Nicaragua, and possibly Cuba—those who are brave enough to oppose Washington's imperial orders.

Nobody can deny that with such a decision, Santos's administration put pressure on the final phase of the Peace Dialogues in Havana, because how could the Colombian insurgency trust in the promises of a government that, in association with NATO, materially supports harmful interventionist and militarist policies in the region? On the other hand, this decision can only weaken ongoing supranational integration and unity processes in Latin America and the Caribbean. The Empire's 'Troy horses' thesis, which we have repeatedly put forward in our texts on this issue, are fortified by the Colombian president's decision. What will UNASUR do now? How can the South American Defense Council act; as their vision, conferred on them by our nations' heads of state, has been to consolidate our region as a Peace Zone; as an area free from the presence of nuclear weapons of mass destruction; and as a contributor to world peace for which a common defence policy and the strengthening of regional cooperation in that field are required? What are the consequences for UNASUR, and broadly speaking for the different policy integration and coordination projects in Latin America, of Colombia joining NATO and adhering to the British position in the conflict on the Malvinas Islands in Argentina?

The peoples of Latin America have dreamed of becoming a denuclearized continent. If, in previous decades, we might have believed it was possible, it is no longer the case. There is evidence that suggests that it is very likely that there are nuclear weapons in the Malvinas Islands, and we ignore the kinds of weapons stored in the seven bases that Washington has in Colombia or on the eleven bases in Peru.[29] The agreements that enabled the installation of

[29] As to the military bases, it is essential to see Telma Luzzani's book, *Territorios vigilados. Cómo opera la red de bases militares norteamericanas en Sudamérica* [Surveilled Territories. How Does the Network of US Military

such bases contain clauses that confer upon the United States the right to enter their bases with military cargo without having to subject it to control by any of the host states. It is not by chance that when, in one of the UNASUR meetings, Chávez requested the organization proceed to verify what was in each of the US bases in the region, he was met with rejection from Álvaro Uribe and Alan García, who were the representatives of the two countries that opened their doors to US military troops and equipment. It is impossible for this continent to achieve peace with eighty US military bases in our countries. These bases are vehicles for war, not for peace. And they will be fully engaged to the extent that the deterioration of the international situation pushes Washington to consolidate its power in its backyard and to suffocate any attempt at national self-determination or democratic progress. We should launch a continental campaign to expel all US bases and those of the United Kingdom, the Netherlands, and France from the region. They will merely bring violence and death, and we, the Latin American and Caribbean people, want peace. It is a reasonable proposal that is supported by political forces and social movements in the region. And our children and the children of our children will never forgive us if we do not do something to put a definitive end to such threats.

Bases Operate in South America?], Buenos Aires: Debate, 2012; and also, the diverse documents of MOPASSOL's work—the Movement for Peace, Sovereignty and Solidarity between Peoples (MoPaSSol), which, when headed by the recently deceased Rina Bertaccini, carried out a significant survey of the foreign military bases established within the region.

REFERENCES

Borón, Atilio. 2012. *América Latina en la geopolítica del imperialismo* [Latin America in the Geopolitics of Imperialism]. Buenos Aires: Ediciones Luxemburg.

———. 2014. *América Latina en la geopolítica del imperialismo* [Latin America in the Geopolitics of Imperialism]. 4th ed. Buenos Aires: Ediciones Luxemburg.

———, and Alexia Massholder. 2014. 'Pensamiento Estratégico Estadounidense' [US Strategic Thought], *Revista de Estudios Estratégicos*, no. 2 (2nd half), pp. 39–52.

Brzezinski, Zbigniew. 2012. *Strategic Vision: America and the Crisis of Global Power*. New York: Basic Books.

Crocker, Chester A. 2015. 'The Strategic Dilemma of a World Adrift'. *Survival*, vol. 57, no. 1 (February–March), pp. 7–30.

Engels, F. (1851) 2010. 'Letter to Weydemeyer'. In *Marx and Engels. Collected Works*. Vol. 38, *Letters. 1844–51*. Digital edition: Lawrence & Wishart.

Fontana, J. 2011. *Por el bien del imperio: Una historia del mundo desde 1945* [For the Good of the Empire: A History of the World Since 1945]. Barcelona: Pasado & Presente.

Klachko, Paula, and Katu Arkonada. 2016. *Desde abajo, desde arriba. De la resistencia a los gobiernos populares: Escenarios y horizontes del cambio de época en América Latina* [From Below, From the Top. From Popular Resistance to the Government. Scenarios and Horizons of a Change of Times in Latin America]. Buenos Aires: Prometeo Libros.

Klare, Michael T. 2012. *The Race for What's Left: The Global Scramble for the World's Last Resources*. New York: Metropolitan Books.

Marx, K. (1857) 2010. *Marx 1857–61*. Vol. 28 of *Marx and Engels. Collected Works*. Digital edition: Lawrence & Wishart.

National Security Strategy. 2015. Washington: The White House.

Nye, Jr., Joseph. 2004. *Soft Power: The Means to Success in World Politics*. New York: Public Affairs.

Obama, Barack. 2014. 'Remarks by the President at the United States Military Academy Commencement Ceremony'. The White House,

Office of the Press Secretary, 28 May. https://obamawhitehouse.archives.gov/the-press-office/2014/05/28/remarks-president-united-states-military-academy-commencement-ceremony, last accessed June 12, 2020.

GABRIEL E. MERINO

THE IMPERIAL RECONFIGURATION OF THE UNITED STATES AGAINST THE RISE OF CHINA[1]

The current historical-spatial transition of the world system manifests itself, among other forms, as a structural capitalist crisis—a crisis of the United States's hegemony and of the world order built by the Anglo-American pole of power. They are different dimensions of the same box. Capitalist accumulation is always related to the political and military power that ensures it. This power determines the rules of the game, builds monopolies for the valorization of value, conquers territories, disciplines rivals, and gains legitimacy. Political and military power nourishes itself with economic power and the unfinished accumulation of value, to obtain the resources for its own extended reproduction. This is the nature of modern imperialism.

The historical transition's geopolitical dimension begins to be clearly perceived around the years 1999–2001, when the contemporary situation of relative multipolarity germinated as a reaction to the Anglo-American neoliberal financial globalization and its political and military expansion. The relative decline of the United States and the 'West' on the one hand, and the re-emergence of China and the Asia Pacific on the other, is one of the main features of the changing times in which we live. It cannot

[1] This work is based on a series of investigations published in Merino (2014, 2017, 2018a, 2018b, 2019) and Merino and Trivi (2019).

be understood only as a hegemonic transition within the modern world system—that is, as part of the succession of hegemonic cycles initiated in the fifteenth century, such as Iberian-Genoese, Dutch, British, American (until now). The re-emergence of China, the rise of Asia Pacific, their alliances with Russia, the growing development of a Eurasian space and the anti-hegemonic resistance driven by forces from the Global South are all expressions of the crisis in the constitutive elements of the modern world system. The crisis is of its Eurocentric or 'Western-centred' feature; its capitalist feature; its particular centre-semiperiphery-periphery order, and the specificity of modern imperialism, which is associated with unfinished capital accumulation and with the resolution of the obstacles to accumulation.

A reverse process is going on these days with respect to what took place in the late-eighteenth and early-nineteenth centuries. Western capitalist imperialism led by the United Kingdom colonized and diminished India and China, which were the largest economies in the world then, and turned them into a periphery. The process has been called 'the Great Divergence'. It was achieved mainly with the expansion of the British Army. We should wonder if we are facing another 'great divergence' now, but in the opposite direction.

About China's rise, the many power groups, led by forces in the US, don't agree on what must be done. This has created the space for adoption of different imperialistic strategies. Giovanni Arrighi (2007, p. 283) points out the different tactics, highlighting first the dominant neoconservative position of George W. Bush's government. The American forces were strong enough to persuade potential contenders in military accumulation hoping to exceed or match United States's power. The focus was on US military supremacy and unilateral interventionism, with control over West Asia and its hydrocarbon resources as a key for global supremacy. Because of this, and especially due to the failure in Iraq (in 2003), three strategies emerged from the neorealist perspective: 1) The restrainment of China through a balance coalition and the establishment of PACOM, a military alliance in Asia Pacific similar to the NATO, formulated by Robert D. Kaplan, and which other scholars extend to the Indian Ocean. 2) The strategy of co-optation and establishment of a stable international system centred on political and economic dimensions, formulated mainly by Henry Kissinger and Zbigniew Brzezinski, which constrain and commit China to maintain the current world order in return for concessions. 3) The 'happy-third' strategy of the US, speculating on China's rivalry with other Asian powers (especially India and Japan) and a neo-Hamiltonian policy of (highly protectionist) industrialization, with focus on defence industries, formulated by Pinkerton.[2] The last can be viewed as two different formulations. Then there is also liberal internationalism, which is centred on the criticism of China's human rights record and, in general, the Chinese leadership's rejection of Western values. Liberalism argues that war is not inevitable and that the establishment of institutions and regulatory standards can control China.

Taking these strategies into account, we propose another perspective here to view the strategic differences of opinion within the United States on the threat posed by China's rise to its dominant global position. This perspective identifies the forces that are in conflict within the US, focusing on the disputes between the globalists and Americanists. We then look at the debates, power groups and vested interests, to identify two major imperialist strategies, with their specific geostrategies, and understand the different ways of dealing with China. On the basis of this analysis,

2 With different nuances and valorizations, the idea of balance of power, characteristic of neorealism, appears in the three strategies with the objective that the United States maintain supremacy in Eurasia and, after that, in the world: '... employ its influence in Eurasia in a manner that creates a stable continental equilibrium with the United States as the political arbiter.' (Brzezinski 1998, p. 11)

we try to understand the ongoing imperialistic reconfigurations since Donald Trump became the US president. Besides, we examine key aspects of China's rise, its geopolitical facets and the Eastern giant's responses to Washington's strategies. Finally, we analyse the current commercial war within the framework of factionalism in the US and the country's geopolitical struggles.

THE EPHEMERAL *BELLE ÉPOQUE* OF UNIPOLAR NEOLIBERALISM

Transformations in the economic field due to growth of transnational financial capital and changes in capitalist relations of production—together with the political, ideological and military offensive of the neoliberal project headed by the US and the UK—enable the reconstruction of American hegemony, more specifically, Anglo-American hegemony. Without a doubt, the fall of the USSR was essential for this. The new growth cycle initiated in 1993–94 left behind the negative cycle of the 1970s, and later, consolidated the short, neoliberal *belle époque.*

The world became unipolar, and 'globalism' emerged as an ideological description of the new stage of global capitalism and also as a political project. Transnationalization of the financial, productive and cultural sectors required a transnational power structure that managed the new global order and solved global capitalism's contradictions. The United States's project to become a global state was unfeasible, but at the same time the scaffold of globalist institutionalism was established and developed at its own base. Key postwar multilateral organizations—the International Monetary Fund (IMF) and World Bank (WB)—were strengthened under the control of the US and the Global North. Moreover, the World Trade Organization (WTO) was created and a set of global standards related to commerce, investment, intellectual property, etc., were launched to impel agreements and institutions.

International courts such as the International Centre for Settlement of Investment Disputes (ICSID) were also established,[3] to arbitrate investment-related differences, taking the power away from nation-states. This globalist institutionality meant a process of weakening national sovereignties and the successive denationalization of nation-states.

However, early symptoms of the crisis began to manifest towards the end of the twentieth century, at the height of the neoliberal *belle époque*. While the Zapatista uprising in south Mexico in 1994 showed the strong impact of the neoliberal financial project on the poor people of the Global South, with the end of Asian financial crisis of 1997–99 and the emergence of popular governments in Latin America, contradictions began to appear among the dominant groups of the system, and the first political and strategic signs of the particular multipolarity of the geopolitical transition could be observed. The reconstruction of American hegemony in the 1980s, and its glory in the 1990s, started to show its own limitations and contradictions: if the so-called globalization, economic transnationalization and links with China were pillars of that reconstruction, these elements contained at the same time the germ of a terminal crisis of American hegemony.

In this sense, at the end of the millennium the BRICS[4] countries appeared to be the arena of the Global North's transnational capital expansion—a new spatial solution for the accumulation of capital, progressively integrated as the semiperiphery in the international institutions of global governance created by the West. But it could also be observed that the developments in certain countries, known as 'emerging' or of the 'Global South', would some years later become an unhappy reality for the establishment that defended the current world order. This is how the Anglo-

3 Belonging to the World Bank.

4 Acronym coined by Jim O'Neal of Goldman Sachs, for whom London was the capital of these emergent markets.

American establishment understands it, as noted in the *Financial Times*:

> Not so long ago, policy makers in the west assumed that China and Russia may eventually decide they wanted to be like 'us'. China would develop as a responsible stakeholder in the existing international order and Russia, albeit with missteps, would see its future in integration with Europe. Xi and Putin have decided otherwise. The world is waking up from the postmodern dreams of global governance to another era of great power competition.[5]

In 1999, led by the US, NATO's unilateral military attack on Yugoslavia and the bombing of the Chinese embassy in Belgrade by US forces, started to show the limits of the belief in 'the end of history'. The same year, China regained control of Macao, which had belonged to Portugal since the sixteenth century and was made its colony in 1887. Just two years prior, China had regained sovereignty over Hong Kong, a British colony since 1842. It was probably the first milestone of the new great divergence, the first one having been initiated with the Opium Wars as a way of subordinating and peripheralizing China. This, together with the formation of the Shanghai Cooperation Organisation with Russia and Central Asian countries (on whose progress the United States had focused), is among the geopolitical displays of change—with China as the protagonist.

Another sign of this change came in April 2001, when China captured a US Navy plane that collided with a Chinese fighter jet over the South China Sea. It gave China access to American surveillance technology and classified information. The incident aggravated the George W. Bush administration and showed

5 Philip Stephens, 'What Xi and Putin really think about the west', *Financial Times*, June 5, 2014.

Beijing's increasing hostility towards the challenges to its territorial sovereignty.

The standoff occurred in the midst of a profound change in the framing of United States's bilateral relations with the Asian giant by the Bush government—shifting from 'strategic association in the twenty-first century' to 'strategic competition'. The implications of the new framework included the possibility that the US would sell modern weapons to the island state of Taiwan—over which China claims sovereignty—and build an anti-missile shield around China.

Moreover, with the framing of 'strategic competition', China began to be seen as a threat in the American backyard because of its increasing commercial influence in Latin America. In 2005, at a hearing entitled 'China's Influence in the Western Hemisphere' before the Subcommittee on the Western Hemisphere of the Committee on International Relations in the US Congress, legislators and officials from the State Department and Pentagon agreed that China's influence was growing every day in Argentina, Brazil, Venezuela and the rest of Latin America. They said it represented 'a "concern" for the development of democracy and human rights in the continent' (Alconada Mon 2005). The Deputy Assistant Secretary Rogelio Pardo-Maurer affirmed being 'worried by the increasing presence of China in the countries of the region' and highlighted that the United States should 'be on the alert' as regards 'certain Chinese activities' (ibid.).

Growing tensions with China since 1999 and changes in the United States, which, as we will later see, are the result of modified power relations in favour of what is known as 'Americanism' in that country, coincides with a set of facts that mark the beginning of the end of the unipolar, neoliberal *belle époque*: 1) The launch of the euro by the continentalist forces of Europe, driven by Berlin and Paris in their quest to become stronger and have more leeway to manoeuvre and face the US, their ally and fundamental 'protector'. 2) Putin's assumption of power in Russia, which will prompt the re-emergence of nationalist forces in the Eurasian giant. 3) The ascent to power of Chávez in Venezuela, which would indicate the break from American hegemony and the Washington Consensus in Latin America, together with the crisis in Brazil that weakened the neoliberal forces in the South American 'giant' and the weakening of power groups and dominant classes in Argentina with the emergence of the Grupo Productivo ('Productive Group'). We should add here the crisis in Ecuador that provoked the dollarization and the Cochabamba 'Water War' (Guerra del agua) in Bolivia in 1999–2000, a key moment in the popular national process that brought the Movimiento al Socialismo (Movement for Socialism; MAS) to power some years later (García Linera 2008). 4) The Jubilee 2000 call by the Catholic Church, proposing to forgive the debt of poor countries and accompanied by a criticism of neoliberalism and unbridled capitalism. It is since then that the early geopolitical manifestations of the crises of American hegemony and the current global order can be observed. They became apparent with the failure of the war in Iraq and with the global financial crisis of 2008.

THE BREAK IN THE US ESTABLISHMENT AND IMPERIALIST DYNAMICS

The change of framework by George W. Bush's government—declaring 'strategic competition' with China—should be interpreted as a factor of the oppositions that exist within the American (and Anglo-American) establishment. The characteristics of the current fissure in the dominant classes and powerful groups of the establishment began to be observed by the end of Clinton's administration, when he promoted, among other issues: a) the repeal of the Glass–Steagall Act, which ended the separation of commercial and investment banking in the

US, creating huge global financial networks; b) the formation of the Group of Twenty (G20) international forum, incited by globalist forces as a new platform for the global governance of transnationalized capitalism; c) the creation and strengthening of multilateral international institutions (such as IMF, WB, WTO) by globalist forces, which according to the Americanists, were detrimental to national sovereignties, even of the United States itself.

With the Bush government in office and the advance of neoconservatism in American foreign policy after the attack on the World Trade Center in 2001, an Americanist reaction was evidenced. It was expressed in the implementation of unilateralism—the G20 was laid aside to return to the older Group of Seven (G7) countries of the Global North (United States, Canada, Western Europe and Japan) and even the Group of Eight (G8), which includes Russia. Moreover, an Anglo-American unilateralism was established at the expense of Clinton's globalist multilateralism. It focused on military supremacy and dominance over West Asia, to ensure the US's hegemonic position in the global order after having strained relations with allies such as France and Germany in the Iraq War (Harvey 2004). Also, the excessive strengthening of multilateral international institutions was dismissed to regain direct power over decisions made by the United States at the expense of the 'global bureaucracy'.[6] At

[6] It is interesting to read an editorial of *Wall Street Journal*, which represents the interest of the forces we call Americanists, commenting on the actions of Argentina's government against the attacks by holdout creditors for restructuring sovereign debt. The editorial supported the American judge Thomas Griesa's remarks in favour of the holdout plaintiffs in the litigation: 'Default is so nonsensical that it raises the question of whether [Argentina's Minister of Economy] Mr Kicillof is inviting it as a way to prod the International Monetary Fund and American liberals to accelerate their campaign to put debt negotiations in the hands of a new global bureaucracy. This would give more leverage to debtors and politicians at the expense of financial markets and US courts' ('Argentina Dances With Default', *Wall*

the same time, by applying military Keynesianism (public deficit and superlative increase of the military budget, legitimated by the war), the Bush administration tried to boost the domestic economy through the military-industrial complex.[7] On the other hand, China was defined as a strategic competitor—a policy that Donald Trump was to take even further later on—preventing Chinese companies from acquiring assets considered strategic by Washington. The most notorious case was the 2005 decision to block the Chinese National Offshore Oil Corporation's subsidiary from buying Unocal, an oil company in California.

With its epicentre in the United States and the United Kingdom, the financial crisis in 2007–08 was another key moment of this struggle within the dominant classes—the financial factions, the globalists and the Americanists (Merino 2014). It was a crisis that revealed the limits of the financialization and the problem of overaccumulation. With Barack Obama's triumph, 'globalism' returned, reinstalling unipolar multilateralism in the government agenda. It meant multilateral trade agreements for commerce and investment; expansionary military alliances in the Eurasian periphery to constrain/prevent the emergence of geopolitical rivals; attempts to strengthen multilateral institutions of the Global North; and the impulse towards multiculturalism as the dominant ideology. The attempts to abandon conventional wars in favour of hybrid wars, colour revolutions and non-conventional wars returned, too. An example of this is the United States executing ten times more drone attacks in territories where it was not formally fighting a war, such as Yemen, Somalia and Pakistan. Also, it

Street Journal, July 28, 2014).

[7] According to World Bank data, after a decade of dropping military expenditure in relation to the total expenditure of the central government in the United States, between 2001 and 2004 it increased from 15.15 per cent to 18.61 per cent which it maintained until 2008 when it started to fall again. As far as the fiscal deficit is concerned, from the 0.58 per cent of the GDP in 2001 it reached 6.68 per cent in 2008 (aggravated by the crisis).

provided support to insurgent forces and colour revolutions in countries where the government was against its interests. Obama's government articulated the dominant programme of transnational financial capital (especially of Anglo-American origin) and the geopolitical interests of the globalist establishment (which tried to include the interests of its allies in Western Europe and Japan). It was done with certain minimum concessions to the popular American classes through focalized programmes and the partial recovery of the liberal agenda in relation to civil rights and individual liberties. But such articulation turned out to be highly contradictory.

For the globalist forces, what is at stake in the current strategic scene is who writes the rules of the game in the twenty-first century. That is, the institutionality that emerges from this historical-spatial transition process should set a new order in the world system, capable of containing defiant poles of power. Such a dispute is crucial given the fact that the geostrategy of the Anglo-American globalist forces is inseparable from the logic of transnational capital in global financial networks. Considering the arguments of Arrighi and Silver (2001) and Harvey (2004), among others, the current capitalist crisis can be 'solved' in its geopolitical dimension only as long as the globalist forces maintain the political and military power that guarantees the accumulation of the Global North's transnational capital. And this establishes a tendency to move towards new globalist institutionality, an impulse towards an impossible global state centred in the United States and the Anglo-American pole of power, and to subordinate/contain the emergent poles that challenge the dominant pole. For this, free trade agreements and military alliances in the Eurasian peripheries (key regions of the Rimland) have been crucial.

As observed by Brzezinski, a neorealist with great influence on the globalists, 'America's global primacy is directly dependent on how long and how effectively its preponderance on the Eurasian continent is sustained' (Brzezinski 1998, p. 39). In this sense, the job was to ensure that no state or group of states (i.e. poles of power) obtained the capacity to expel the United States from Eurasia or limit its role as arbiter. And for this, free trade agreements in the western and eastern peripheries of Eurasia became essential. By 2014, such agreements became even more crucial with the weakening of the United States, the global hegemonic crisis, the capitalist crisis centred in the West, the challenge of emergent powers, the awakening of the East, the great progress of China, and the fight for control of the Pacific as the centre of accumulation on a global scale.

As an expression of this geostrategy, which pretended to lead and involve all the forces of what is geopolitically known as 'West' and geoeconomically as 'Global North', Hillary Clinton (2011) asserted that the future of world politics would be decided in Asia and the Pacific, not in Afghanistan or Iraq—as the neoconservatives had claimed—and the United States should be at the centre of the action. Clinton, who was Obama's Secretary of State, added that the strategic axis of the American foreign policy should go from the 'Atlantic to the Pacific'. Also, she stated the necessity of generating an alliance similar to NATO in the Pacific, which could include the Indian Ocean, i.e. mainly India, perhaps operationalized by the United States Indo-Pacific Command.

From this point of view, the globalist forces emphasized two key instruments: the Trans-Pacific Partnership (TPP) and the Transatlantic Trade and Investment Partnership (TTIP). The TPP[8] would have had an important geopolitical impact in terms of the distribution of power in the Asia Pacific, as the interest of the United States was to maintain a favourable balance in such regions

[8] While the Trans-Pacific Partnership was signed in February 2016, the US withdrew from it in January 2017 after the election of Donald Trump. The remaining countries have since negotiated a different trade agreement without the United States.—*Ed.*

and constrain/surround China. This explains why the globalist forces insisted on 'protecting' some states such as the Philippines, Vietnam and Taiwan from greatly depending on the Chinese economy, for them not to lose their independent diplomatic and political influence.

In the case of the TTIP, the agreement to move forward in Eurasia's western periphery together with the NATO, the substantive issue was whether Atlanticism should dominate, reinforcing the globalist position.[9] The Eurasian threats, the global crisis situation and the new challenge of emerging powers appear repeatedly in the discussions of globalist Atlanticists in favour of TTIP. At a dialogue on TTIP in Stockholm in 2016, Michael Froman (US Trade Representative) pointed out that there was no 'Plan B' if the TTIP negotiations did not conclude that year. He added: 'We either work together to help set the rules of the world or we leave that role to others.' As the analyst and former US Navy admiral and NATO supreme allied commander James Stavridis observed in an article for *Foreign Policy*, going on with the TTIP would 'more tightly bind Europe to the United States, thus hurting Russian leverage. The TTIP is a sensible agreement on economic grounds, broadly speaking. But it also holds enormous real value in the geopolitical sphere' (Stavridis 2014).

In case the TPP and the TTIP had come into effect the globalist forces, whose essential core is Anglo-Saxon territoriality, would have been able to lay down a territorial basis for 51 countries, with 1.6 billion people and two thirds of the world GDP, counting on a powerful critical mass, to go through the struggle for reconfiguration of the world order. It would have consolidated its power in some crucial aspects, starting with control of the western

[9] The Transatlantic Trade and Investment Partnership negotiations were likewise halted by the Trump administration. Though talks had resumed in 2018, by mid-2019 the EU declared them 'obsolete and no longer relevant'.—*Ed.*

and eastern peripheries of Eurasia, to weaken the development of a Eurasian block. It would have reinforced an aligned Europe in the Atlantic, China would have been constrained in its global and regional expansion and influence, and Russia would be more isolated. Meanwhile, in Latin America, the Pacific Alliance—a regional form of the TPP—would move forward and the free market agreements between the European Union and Mercosur—the Southern Common Market, a South American trade bloc—would fall under the paradigm of open regionalism, which is to the detriment of the attempt to constitute a regional power bloc.

However, with Brexit, first, and then Donald Trump's triumph over Hillary Clinton, the globalist forces were politically defeated in their own territories. This accompanied the *deglobalization* impasse, which has been expressed in the world economy since 2010, when the formula of the so-called economic globalization—i.e. with each point of GDP growth, foreign trade increased by two points and foreign direct investment by three—was exhausted.

During the presidential campaign in 2016 we could observe that the political fight in the United States was inherently intertwined with the current capitalist crisis,[10] and the loss of relative power on the international scene (two sides of the same coin) showed a hegemonic link between the dominant factions. This is expressed in deep polarization on every topic, fostering the construction of a strategic political project: 1) the war in Iraq and the strategy in West Asia; 2) the role and power of multilateral organizations and institutions such as IMF, WB, WTO, etc., in relation to the role and state power of the United States (unipolar unilateralism vs unipolar multilaterism); 3) the strategy for confronting emergent regional and global forces or poles of power; 4) the multilateral

[10] Neo-Keynesians like Larry Summers, former Treasury secretary (1999–2001) and director of National Economic Council (2009–10) of the US, refer to and conceptualize the crisis as a phase of secular stagnation (Summers 2014).

agreements for trade, investment and transnational economic regulation (TPP, TTIP, NAFTA); 5) reforms in the regulation of the financial system; 6) the value of the US Federal Reserve's benchmark interest rate and its general monetary policy; 7) the issue of climate change; 8) dedication to hybrid or conventional wars, etc. And these polarizations cross intellectual debate, articulating different theoretical perspectives and even breaking such perspectives in different ways.

Within the establishment, there is an agreement to maintain unipolarity, and, in this sense, together face the emergent poles of power that challenge the situation, especially China and Russia, and keep the establishment's allies subordinated. They share the three great imperatives in the imperial geostrategy: to avoid clashes among serfs and maintain their dependency on security; to keep obedient and protected subordinates; and to prevent the barbarians from coming together (Brzezinski 1998). However, they differ on *how* to do it, and that has structural roots. On the other hand, as such struggles persist they unify in the state, producing a particular political result with strategic continuities between different political positions. But at the same time this means that multiple contradictory policies exist within the state and the bureaucracy is also polarized, giving place to an intense courtiers' struggle.

TRUMP AND HIS RETURN TO UNILATERAL IMPERIALISM

The triumph of Donald Trump in the presidential race indicates a qualitatively greater moment in the struggle for power in the United States. It indicates the reaction of a group of actors that found themselves threatened or harmed in the process of globalization, i.e. the specific phase of the historical process of internationalization of the world system. The tension of the moment was heightened by the steepest decline of the US and the capitalist crisis that exacerbated the fight between capitalists, affecting important categories of workers and business factions. Trump therefore went beyond the classic conservative and neoliberal agenda of the Republican Party elite, incorporating more elements of industrial economic nationalism and an anti-establishment discourse. He picked a clear side in favour of Brexit and he went against NAFTA, TPP and TTIP, trying to turn commercial relations into a bilateral relation in order to impose the weight of the American economy and its arbitrary political power, to avoid competition that is 'harmful' to disadvantaged groups and branches (especially to the capital of allied countries), sharpening protectionist practices.[11]

On the other hand, Trump's government resumed the foreign policy of Bush and the neoconservatives which spoke of the 'axis of evil', which included Iran, Iraq, North Korea, Libya, Syria and Cuba at first, and to which Belarus, Myanmar and Zimbabwe were added. The potential for wars in those secondary territories meets the objective of conquering key geopolitical positions and/or preventing the advance of rival powers. At the same time, they sustain the domestic American economy through the military-industrial complex, using the dollar's monopoly to

[11] The two faces of this 'globalization' process are evident: on the one hand, since the mid-1980s, the profits of the American companies have increased inordinately. In particular, the profits made in other countries compared to profits obtained in the United States. They went from 50 billion dollars to 500 billion dollars in 2008, exceeding the volume of domestic profits. In contrast, the process saw 60,000 companies in the US in bankruptcy, low growth of productivity in the SME sector between 2010 and 2017 in relation to the most dynamic core, a destruction of 5 million industrial jobs during the last 15 years, a fall of the wage share over the GDP from 48.7 per cent (1980) to 42.7 per cent (2015), and the emergence of the phenomenon of 'super-exploitation' of the labour force, creating a constant landscape of the creative destruction of capital's 'satanic mills'.

finance it. Besides, it presents clear support to the neoconservative geostrategy of Benjamin Netanyahu's government in Israel (conveyed by the relocation of the American embassy from Tel Aviv to Jerusalem), which implies moving on without regard to the conquest of Palestine and the construction of Greater Israel to destabilize regional powers. Also, the return to marking Iran as the great enemy to defeat in the geopolitically crucial Greater Middle East is observed, which raises the imperative of destroying the nuclear deal between Iran and the major world powers.

At the same time, a change from the Bush administration's stance is seen in the military doctrine, keeping in line with the current world situation where confrontation with rival states threatening US's global domain, especially China and Russia, is central. Furthermore, unilateralism has intensified under Trump's government, as observed in the breach of agreements with Iran and Cuba, withdrawal from the Paris Agreement, tensions in NATO, the trade war involving allies, the crisis in the WTO and questioning of its dispute system, the transfer of the American embassy to Jerusalem, and the US's withdrawal from UNESCO. The world order, built mainly by the United States, is, paradoxically, questioned by the forces vying for power in the United States. The globalists understand that it is already obsolete and insufficient to constrain emerging powers and the new reality of global power, while the Americanists and nationalists understand that the world order has turned against them and has become an obstacle in the strategy to regain supremacy.

In the case of Latin America, Trumpism takes up the fight for direct hegemonic control of the region as a priority to influence confrontation with other power blocs. Vice President Mike Pence invoked the Monroe Doctrine—'America for the Americans'—to warn other nations from interfering in South America, and former national security advisor John Bolton asserted that such a doctrine was 'alive and well'.[12] These personalities, together with Secretary of State Mike Pompeo and other neoconservatives, have intensified the pressure on Cuba, Venezuela and Nicaragua. Moreover, Admiral Kurt Tidd, former commander of the United States Southern Command, has consistently pointed out, with special concern, Beijing's influence—as well as Russia's and Iran's—in Latin America, and its geoeconomic progress as the main trade partner in South America, terming their interventions as a threat to US national security.[13] In this sense, Washington explicitly implements the spheres-of-influence policy. As observed by Borón (2014), although the region is always a priority for American imperialism, an important change of strategy can be identified from Trump onwards. For example, if we just take into account Cuba and observe the agreements and Obama's 'Cuban thaw' policy, and compare it to the axis-of-evil policy—the absolute blockade and sanctions of Trump's government—they are two very different imperialist strategies, which are also seen in the case of Iran.

As regards the current political phase, Americanism claims a return to sovereignty of the nation-state and the unilateral strength of the Anglo-American pole of power—together with the United Kingdom, Canada, Australia, New Zealand, and Israel. This is why Brexit and the strengthening of economic ties among those countries become important. The reinforcement of what we can call 'unilateral Anglo-Americanism' in the geopolitical sphere corresponds to an identitarian Anglo-Saxonism as the strategic horizon, which in its dominant form is expressed as supremacy, an aggravation of the white, Anglo-Saxon, Protestant identity (or

12 'Consejero de Seguridad de la Casa Blanca reafirma la vigencia de la Doctrina Monroe' [White House Security Adviser Reaffirms the Validity of the Monroe Doctrine], *Sputnik*, April 18, 2019.

13 Statement to the Senate Armed Services Committee by Admiral Kurt W. Tidd, Commander, US Southern Command, February 15, 2018.

'WASP'). It acts as the mortar for reverse imperialism, showing itself in politics as a kind of ethnic nationalism.

These changes initiated by Trump have an economic and social anchor. While in the political sphere globalism tends to institutionalize Western transnationalized power, in the cultural sphere multiculturalism undermines national identities in Western liberalized countries. In the economic sphere, globalism reconfigures the old centre, develops new global centre-nodes and creates new peripheries out of the old centres. In this sense, the so-called 'rust belt' emerged as a new periphery in the United States, of what used to be the industrial heart of the Midwest, similar to the British Midland, whose voters mainly turned in favour of Trump and Brexit. The manufacturing capitals that dominate in the domestic market, which are less competitive in international terms, see themselves succumbing to the intensification of competition and competitive capital concurrence. Besides, the industrial progress of China sharpens the competitive pressures and broadens the space for global capital accumulation, intensifying competition and fusion among capitals. This is reinforced because the American state has difficulties in maintaining monopoly conditions. Because of this, the forces opposed to globalism also reject the TPP and the TTIP and target their own allies, from whom they demand unilateral subordination, intensifying, necessarily, the struggles within the Global North.

The fight between capitals and the processes of crises feed the political-strategic struggles (capitalist models in conflict, geostrategies in conflict, identities and worldviews in conflict, etc.) and constitutes a central element in analysing fissures within the United States and the Anglo-American pole. In this sense, it is not incidental that Trump receives major support from the coal industry and the American steel and metal industries. Dan DiMicco, former CEO of Nucor steel industry was one of Trump's main advisors on trade and economic policy. Robert Lighthizer, nominated as the US Trade Representative by Trump, has a long history representing the American steel industry and he has promoted the protectionist shift in important sectors in the Republican Party. He had also led the steel industry battles against Japan decades ago.

This industry presence in Trump's government is strengthened by personalities like Mike Pompeo, closely related to Koch industries, as the Secretary of State, as well as Secretary of Defense Mark Thomas Esper, who was vice president of government relations at Raytheon, a major US defence contractor. Esper had taken over his role at the Pentagon from Patrick Shanahan, who had worked at Boeing aerospace company in various capacities between 1986 and 2017.

Therefore, it is not strange that one of Trump's first decisions, in line with his own protectionist promises, was to order the Department of Commerce to investigate if steel imports, particularly those from China, were a threat to US national security. Flanked by representatives of the steel industry, Trump said: 'Steel is fundamental for both our economy and our Armed Forces. This is not an area where we can allow ourselves to depend on foreign countries.'[14] He meant that protecting the industry was a matter of national security. Thus, a key group from the military-industrial complex was made dominant in the executive with Trump.

Another issue referred to in the economic agenda, which caused conflict between top US companies, was about the border tax or import tax announced by the Trump administration as part of its fiscal reform. When it was proposed, 16 large US companies wrote a letter urging the US Congress to adopt the import tax. The letter was signed by executives of Boeing, CoorsTek, Caterpillar,

14 'Trump ordena investigar si las importaciones de acero amenazan la seguridad nacional' [Trump Orders Investigation Into Whether Steel Imports Threaten National Security], Agencia EFE, April 20, 2017. Quoted text translated from Spanish.

Dow Chemical Co, Celanese Corp, GE, Celgene Corp, Eli Lilly and Co, Raytheon Co, Merck & Co, S&P Global Inc, Oracle Corp, United Technologies Corp, Pfizer Inc, and Varian Medical Systems Inc. These companies have great production capacities in the United States. Some are big contractors of the Pentagon and they see their subsidiaries being affected by global competition, while the American state can no longer guarantee a monopoly.

TRUMP'S TRADE WAR

Trump has declared a trade war on the world. With that, there has been a deepening of the protectionist policy of the United States and along with it, commercial bilateralism has risen to protect different factions of capital and backward branches of the global economy and to strengthen the industrial production of the United States against China's and of allies like Germany, Japan and Mexico. The objective was to rebalance the trade deficit, which was aggravated by the economic stimulus policies of the Trump administration and its military Keynesianism. Above all, it was to reinforce national security, since industry is the basis for defence, and to ensure American technological monopoly against rivals, a key aspect in world power (Amin 1998). In his State of the Union speech Trump emphatically promised major investments in technologies of strategic importance.

At the end of Trump's first year as president, the trade deficit had increased from the previous year (2016). The deficit with China was about 375,168 million dollars, and so Trump's government demanded that China reduce 100 billion dollars in its exports, trying to imitate Ronald Reagan's government in the 1980s when it was obligated to limit Japan's exports, to conform to the Federal Reserve's monetary policy and to finance the Treasury. The problem is that China is not an American political-military protectorate like Japan is; the scale of its economy is much greater (China's GDP has overtaken the United States's in terms of purchasing power parity) and China's alliance with Russia strengthens its political and strategic position in Eurasia.

The key reason for the trade war with China is to stop its drastic global rise. For this, Trumpism considers that it should stop the 'alarming' 'Made in China 2025' policy. Among the main objectives of the policy is to focus on fundamental branches of technology such as robotics, semiconductors and the aerospace industry, and to expand leadership in others, like artificial intelligence and electric car manufacturing. If China's plan materializes, it would definitely, although partially, break up the centre-semiperiphery relationship of the Asian giant with the Global North, creating a crisis in the global division of labour and the hierarchies of the world's economy at the same time that it would present a systemic challenge—a country with a fifth of the world's population becoming the developed centre.

What is at stake for Trumpism is the US's geopolitical primacy in the long run. This was discussed by the intellectual and advisor to Trump, and the current Director of Trade and Industrial Policy, Peter Navarro, in his book *Death by China: Confronting the Dragon – A Global Call to Action* (2011). America's primacy can just be achieved through a twenty-first-century equivalent of Alexander Hamilton's *Report on Manufactures* from 1791—to decide which industries are essential for national security along with a technological-industrial policy that ensures the vital industries remain in the country, complemented by strong protectionism and an economic war against rivals. Pinkerton's economic nationalism, mentioned above, combined with neoconservatism, appears in Navarro's book.

The trade war has its background in the growing economic 'war', in which struggles between the capitals mediated by the states are sharpened. In the context of low growth in the Global North since the global financial crisis of 2007–08, this situation and perspectives on it have deepened. Since there is low growth, the accumulation of particular capitals is against the less developed ones, and workers, affecting the mechanisms of accumulation by dispossession. Global capitals accumulate in emerging territories that are growing (particularly China), but the same is not possible for the capitals that depend on the American national economy. At the same time, the process known as economic globalization halted when the crisis broke out in 2008, which showed a structural limit of neoliberal globalization.

The meagre growth in the Global North in the last few years occurred thanks to the expansionary policies of the central banks. That policy is encountering its limits, creating an enormous bubble in public bonds, which may possibly blow up in one or two years. A near crisis can be observed, which can unfold into a much deeper crisis cycle because of the exhaustion of the expansive Kondratiev cycle initiated in 1994 and the structural tendencies of the world's economy. This predicts a sharpening of the economic struggle that—depending on how it develops and 'ends'—is going to feed the gap in the United States, the global economic war and the struggle between poles of power at all levels.

CHINA'S RISE

China's rise and its economic dynamism are not reducible, as far as we understand it, to its adherence to neoliberal capitalism and/or as an epiphenomenon of globalization and the productive dislocation of the Global North, as considered by a great part of the Western academy. Its rise is closely related, firstly, to the securing of important levels of autonomy and political and military strength (sovereignty) and some basic welfare in terms of health and education because of the revolution in 1949; then the launch, with the reforms initiated in 1978, that attracted the capitals of the Chinese diaspora and absorbed lower levels of the process of outsourcing in the Asia Pacific led by Japan, developed important communal economy and state links and, later, absorbed great volumes of Western capital under its own conditions (planned productive needs, technological transfers, profit extraction constraints), to become, finally, the world's great industrial platform. This was a project of its own, because of its history and specific characteristics—more centred on productivity growth than in capital investment (Zhu 2012)—and with a particular combination of modes of production, taking advantage of the expansive need of the capital of the Global North.

The hybrid development model of China does not qualify within the classic Western capitalist frame, since it maintains collective property of land and the focal points of the economy are in the hands of the state's strategic companies, with robust growth of publicly-owned township and village enterprises (TVEs) which are the main employers in the economy. Thus, the current historical-spatial transition would not be (if it materializes) about a transfer of power from an occidental and capital state to a stronger and more dynamic one, to initiate a new hegemonic cycle of the modern world system. Moreover, China's rise invites us to think about the existence of a definitive and structural tendency—of the end of the primacy of the fundamental forces of the West in the world system and, especially, its supremacy, starred by the Anglo-Saxon world, due to what is considered the great divergence between the early and mid-nineteenth century, with a combination of the industrial revolution, capitalist expansion, colonialism and military supremacy. This is articulated in Wallerstein's formulation (2006) about the fact that we now face a situation that presents a structural limit for the survival of the world's modern system, as it is. The question arises whether we are witnessing a definitive crisis of capitalist modernity as a historical system, and to what extent is the rise of China and the Asia Pacific a part of that process.

As we pointed out at the beginning of the paper, by the end of the unipolar neoliberal *belle époque*, China began to show signs of a new pole of power that could challenge the world order. A key moment of China's rise was the 2008 crisis that hit the Global North, which exposed all of its contradictions. From then on, China stopped financing the US Treasury and its structural deficit through bond purchase. While China bought 49.3 per cent of US Treasury bonds between 2005 and 2008, it acquired only 19.6 per cent in 2009, when facing recession. The rest were destined to feed the impulse response to domestic demand and impede a recession, with funds worth 500 billion dollars being injected into the US economy (Martins 2011). This makes China different from 1980s' Japan, which, as an American military 'protectorate', accepted the deflationist policies of the 'strong dollar' to finance the American deficit and even 'limit itself' in its exports to the United States. Something similar is demanded now by Donald Trump, which China does not deign to accept.

On the other hand, another answer to US hegemony since 2009 was the call for the first meeting of the BRICS, in which space for the main emergent powers—and not just emerging markets—began to be delineated. This showed, among other concerns, the need to collectively move forward towards an alternative to the dollar, a challenge that goes straight to the heart of American hegemony.

As regards China's economic rise, there are three key points to take note of since the crisis in 2008:

1) The acquisition of companies abroad and investments in critical areas for their development needs, linked mainly to energy, food and infrastructure. For example, the purchase by Chinese state-owned grain trading company, COFCO, of the Noble Group and Nidera (of Dutch and Argentinian capitals), which enabled China to consolidate itself as one of the main players in the monopoly of the grain trade. On the other hand, Bright Food, which belongs to the local government of Shanghai, acquired the

British brand Weetabix, and in 2015 bought the Catalan company Miquel Alimentación. We must also highlight, among other acquisitions, the purchase of Swiss biotechnological giant Syngenta for 43 billion dollars, which gave the Chinese access to leading-edge food technology. Or the purchase of Volvo by the Chinese Geely, which gave access to leading-edge automotive technology. A recent attempt to buy US companies producing semiconductor technology, to develop the technological branch, in which China is highly dependent, was forbidden by American authorities.

2) The internationalization of the yuan (renminbi), the increasing use of the yuan as the reserve currency of different central banks, as well as loan agreements in yuans with central banks to strengthen reserves (currency swaps). The World Gold Council certified that in 2016 China and Russia had become, for the sixth consecutive year, the main gold buyers of the world, substantially increasing their reserves in this metal. This is closely related to the policy of propping up their currencies and going back to some form of the gold standard, at the expense of the dollar. Also, the launching of an oil market in yuans reinforces the policy of currency internationalization and hits the valued monopoly of the petrodollar. This was expressed with the creation of new international financial instruments like the Asian Infrastructure Investment Bank and launch of the BRICS New Development Bank and a reserve fund (under the Contingent Reserve Agreement), at the summit in Fortaleza, Brazil, in 2014. This financial architecture is developing in parallel with the Global North's, which is centred on the IMF and WB.

3) The advance towards economic complexity and technological development, where China has already reduced a great part of its disadvantage with the centres of the Global North, and has even begun to be the vanguard in some sectors. According to the data provided by World Bank, China is the largest goods-exporting country in the world, of which 94.4 per cent are manufactured

goods and 48 per cent are machines. And among the manufactured goods, 25.6 per cent are high-tech goods (in 2015). On the other hand, almost 731 million Chinese citizens were online in 2016 and 95 per cent of them had internet access on their mobile phones. This brings us a mass of digital information—Big Data—that is much larger than the American data. It is from this intervention with the giant database that it gained leadership in artificial intelligence (AI), the decisive technology of the current industrial revolution. Besides, Shenzhen or Beijing contend with Silicon Valley and other centres of the Global North with respect to the position of the strategic node of high technology in the world's economy. In fact, Shenzhen, Guangdong, Hong Kong and Macao are part of the Greater Bay Area and the Pearl River Delta, a megalopolis of 70 million inhabitants making 90 per cent of the electronic devices used by the entire world. In this regard, the technological and industrial development plan, 'Made in China 2025', should also be mentioned. It seeks to end the still-existing gap with the Global North in some advanced technological branches (semiconductors, robotics, aerospace technology), and to consolidate its leadership in others.

Hand in hand with its economic growth, China has developed its military complex and modernized its armed forces at high speed. This, together with the power of Russia in this sphere, threatens the American monopoly. China's military budget has increased progressively over the last decade and more, reaching 130 billion dollars in 2014 and exceeding 220 billion in 2017. It is the second highest military budget in the world, although still far below that of the United States.[15] One of the main aspects of Chinese

15 Military expenditure in the world reached its highest level in 2017 since the end of the Cold War, in a year when United States, China and Saudi Arabia were the ones that invested the most in defence, according to an investigation by the Stockholm International Peace Research Institute (SIPRI). United States accounts for 35 per cent of the global military expenditure, China 13 per cent, Saudi Arabia 4 per cent, Russia 3.8 per cent and India 3.7 per cent

military development has to do with the dispute for the control of the Pacific. In this scenario, China intensifies the construction of aircraft carriers, submarines and missiles, strengthening the strategic capacity of its military-industrial complex. According to the Chinese General Sun Sijing, 'The double-digit increase in defence spending may seem too much to some, but in the development of the military complex we are still far behind. Our companies have taken over the world market and we have what and who to defend.'[16] The situation in the waters next to China exacerbated because of the sharpening of global tensions and the geostrategic conflicts around the islands of Senkaku/Diaoyu, the Spratly archipelago and the Paracel Islands, apart from the historical conflict of the Koreas. The South China Sea is essential for the Asian economy. A third of the ships of the world navigate its waters and enormous oil and gas reserves lie below its seabed.[17]

Another key aspect to China's rise is the geopolitical one, together with its geostrategic imperatives. There, a fundamental intention highlights itself: the so-called 'New Silk Road'. The progress of the Trans-Pacific Partnership during Obama's administration and the accession of Japan to the TPP in May 2013 implied a surrounding of China and the move forward in the strategy of constraining its expansion and influence in the Asia Pacific. Against this, the Asian giant answered in September 2013 with the promotion of the Belt and Road Initiative (BRI), trying

(*La Nación*, May 3, 2018).

16 Fragments of the interview of the Political Commissar of the Academy of Military Sciences, General Sun Sijing, have been published in newsletters in China and then by the state-owned channel CCTV ('¿Se prepara China para una guerra con Japón y Occidente?' [Is China Preparing for a War With Japan and the West?], *Russia Today*, September 29, 2014; quoted text translated from Spanish).

17 On its part, Japan (a strategic ally of the United States), increased defence expenditure significantly and modified the interpretation of its 'Peace Constitution' to be able to fight abroad and defend its allies, even when Japan is not under attack. This constituted a historic shift in its foreign policy.

to consolidate, above everything, its power within the heart of the Eurasian continent, facing the challenges of the US–Japan 'sea empire'. Its interest converges with Russia's, increasingly inclined towards the construction of an axis of power anchored in the Eurasian space, against the United States and allies (NATO) in territories considered sensitive to their interests (Eastern Europe, the Caucasus, Central Asia, Syria). The BRI, promoted by Xi Jinping in 2013 after his trips to Russia, Belarus and Kazakhstan (protagonists of the Eurasian Economic Union with its centre in Moscow), involves 60 countries, most of them developing countries. They contain 4.4 billion inhabitants (63 per cent of the world's population), 75 per cent of the known energy reserves of the world and account for 55 per cent of the world's GDP. The Chinese government intends to invest the enormous amount of 1.4 trillion dollars in BRI. A budget of 890 billion dollars is already contemplated, which will come from the Silk Road Fund, the New Development Bank and the Asian Infrastructure Investment Bank. At the same time, the Chinese state-owned commercial banks—Bank of China, ICBC and China Construction Bank—have offered more than 500 billion in loans and asset investments (Parra Pérez 2017).

The three corridors of the BRI seem to have clear geostrategic intentions: to avoid the constraints to the development of China and avoid the Anglo-American geostrategy that surrounds/restrains China, Russia and continental allies, which leaves China with its main lines of supply threatened, vulnerable and blocked. In this sense, on the map where the corridors and the sea routes are drawn, we see that the BRI breaks China's bottlenecks: A train through Myanmar provides a route to the sea that eliminates the congestion point of the Malacca Strait in Singapore (a global financial centre allied to the West). On the other hand, a corridor next to a new port in Pakistan provides direct access to the Indian Ocean and the Persian Gulf, from where comes 40 per cent of the world's traded oil, a great part of which goes to China.[18] Likewise, both, the China–Mongolia–Russia and the New Eurasian Land Bridge corridors enable a direct connection with Europe, an access to the Mediterranean and a continental Eurasian integration. This breaks the buffer that divides Asia Pacific and Europe territorially, which gives strategic territorial superiority to the pole of power that controls the sea. Besides, Russia's protagonism allows it to reduce possible geopolitical misgivings about China's rise. Moreover, the Indochinese corridor would eliminate any threat in continental Southeast Asia.

The development of the Eurasian railway to communicate and integrate the whole continental mass is one of the key elements that stands out in the proposal of the BRI: the projection of a huge Eurasian land bridge that dismantles the maritime power historically held by Western empires of the modern period. In fact, one of the most brilliant thinkers of the Anglo-Saxon sea empire, Halford Mackinder, had already observed the implications for the balance of power of the transcontinental railway in Eurasia at the beginning of the twentieth century:

> A generation ago steam and the Suez Canal appeared to have increased the mobility of sea-power relative to land-power. Railways acted chiefly as feeders to ocean-going commerce. But trans-continental railways are now transmuting the conditions of land-power, and nowhere can they have such effect as in the closed heartland of Euro-Asia ... Is not the pivot region of the world's politics that vast area of Euro-Asia which is inaccessible to ships, but in antiquity lay open to the

18 Parra Pérez (2017, p. 8) points out that 'An important aspect is that the depth of the Port of Gwadar allows to accommodate submarines and aircraft carriers, becoming a reference point in the military strategy of China overseas. This military base and the one in Djibouti show the growing interest of China to increase its deployment beyond the waters of the Pacific-Asia, competing with the American military bases in the region'.

> horse-riding nomads, and is to-day about to be covered with a network of railways? (Mackinder [1904] 2010, pp. 315–16)

In geoeconomic terms, the BRI is part of a global change and means a movement towards the conformation of a new development pattern, different from the one of the triad and its centre-periphery model that, because of its characteristics, tends to the diversification of capital flows and spatial flows of factors of production, which expand progressively and deeply within the Eurasian hinterlands (Ning and Chuankai 2018). The BRI implies the shaping of a radical transformation of the world as it has been configured since the nineteenth century, with its centre in the Atlantic and the West—and its twentieth-century version, especially since the Second World War, with the centre in the United States, where the two other economic centres of the world capitalist system are coordinated, i.e. Western Europe and Japan/ Asia Pacific. From the perspective of the BRI, the geoeconomic centre is China, which as long as it belongs to Eurasia and its eastern and western dynamic peripheries, leaves the United States in a subordinate role and consolidates its strategic maxim of global power construction: 'The middle kingdom is (should be) at the centre of everything that shines under the sky'. This conception differs from the militarist imperialism of the Western type.

CONCLUDING REMARKS

The change of government in the United States, which weakened the globalist forces, enabled China to move forward in geoeconomic terms and even include Japan in the BRI. This new world's political moment was reflected in the Belt and Road Forum held in May 2017 where more than 1,200 delegates from 130 countries and 29 Heads of State attended together with 70 international organizations. Xi Jinping's position in Davos, where he defended the trade liberalization and investment against American protectionism since the Trump administration, is also a sample of China's rise. As has historically happened with big industrial powers, once they reach a certain level of relative development and competition, becoming new centres of the global economy, they replace protectionist positions with positions which are closer to the free market.

However, the negative effects of the trade war on China's economy, the aggressiveness of Washington to prevent the technological advance of China (Huawei being a case in point) and the development of a number of geostrategic tensions around it present great challenges to that rise. Beijing needs to ensure supplies of raw materials and energy that the current government of the United States seems ever ready to restrict. Thus, among other issues, the United States tries to control the Middle East or block China's investment in Latin America. Besides, China must solve problems of overaccumulation of capital and over-capacity of production—it has an important over-capacity in the production of several goods, steel and cement, among others—that can lead it to deploy an accumulation by dispossession that would dynamite its strategic conception and further to the development of a capitalist imperialism similar to the West. Also, it must defend its lines of commerce but it faces the challenge of the United States, which is still the 'dominant military power in Asia and whose navy has the capacity of blocking ports and Chinese maritime traffic using the strategic advantage that its bases offer surrounding Chinese periphery in Japan, Korea and Guam' (Mackinlay Ferreirós 2011, p. 3). Apart from the United States, China is surrounded by powers that look at its rise with suspicion and Washington seeks to make them confront each other, to which we can add a number of key territorial conflicts in the China Sea.

On the other hand, there are deeper challenges to China's rise and the Asia Pacific. We can mention two of the most important, which are closely linked: the impossibility of incorporating a sixth part of the world's population to the centre of the system because of the structural pattern of unequal and combined development inherent to the modern world system (which has also almost collapsed); at the same time, the impossibility of such incorporation within current consumption patterns and the exploitation of nature without sliding into an environmental abyss.

The imperial reconfiguration of the United States and the 'internal' factions against China's rise are a characteristic of the changing times we are living in. Each force tries to face the decline of the United States within their strategic perspectives, shaped in relation to their interests. Within Trump's government we observe the strategic focus to a neo-Hamiltonian economic nationalism of the Pinkerton variety combined, as we have seen, with guidelines typical of neoconservatism that seek to control the Middle East, maintain unilateralism and absolute military supremacy—embodied in the figures of the former Ambassador to UN John Bolton, the Secretary of State Mike Pompeo and Vice President Mike Pence. Also, there appear to be attempts to reinforce the military alliances in the Indo-Pacific zone (with India, Taiwan) and intervene in the main geostrategic conflicts in the region. On the other hand, the neorealist vision of constraint, multilateralism and balance of power, which is closer to the globalists, has been displaced.

Paradoxically, while the current management of the United States might be the most favourable to China's rise—in fact, it is almost giving it key Eurasian allies like Russia, Iran, Turkey and Germany on a silver platter—it is at the same time the most dangerous one. We do not know how far the escalation towards war can go, not only at the level of trade, but at the military level as well.

REFERENCES

Alconada Mon, Hugo. 2005. 'Por las alianzas comerciales de Pekín. Preocupa a EE.UU. la influencia de China en América latina' [Beijing's Business Alliances. US Concerned About China's Influence in Latin America], *La Nación*, Buenos Aires, April 7.

Amin, Samir. 1998. *El capitalismo en la era de la globalización* [Capitalism in the Age of Globalization]. Buenos Aires: Paidos.

Arrighi, Giovanni. 2007. *Adam Smith en Pekín: Orígenes y fundamentos del siglo XXI* [Adam Smith in Beijing: Origins and Foundations of the Century]. Madrid: Akal.

Arrighi, Giovanni, and Beverly Silver. 2001. *Caos y Orden en el Sistema-Mundo Moderno* [Chaos and Governance in the Modern World-System]. Madrid: Akal.

Borón, A. 2014. *América Latina en la geopolítica del imperialismo* [Latin America in the Geopolitics of Imperialism]. Buenos Aires: Ediciones Luxemburg.

Brzezinski, Zbigniew. 1998. *El gran tablero mundial. La supremacía estadounidense y sus imperativos geoestratégicos* [The Grand Chessboard: American Primacy and Its Geostrategic Imperatives]. Buenos Aires: Paidós.

Clinton, Hillary. 2011. 'America's Pacific Century'. *Foreign Policy*, October 11.

García Linera, Álvaro. 2008. 'El Estado en transición: Bloque de poder y punto de bifurcación' [The State in Transition: Power Bloc and Fissures]. In *La potencia plebeya*, pp. 521–26. Buenos Aires: Prometeo Libros.

Harvey, David. 2004. *El Nuevo Imperialismo* [The New Imperialism]. Madrid: Akal.

Mackinder, Halford. (1904) 2010. 'El pivote geográfico de la historia' [The Geographical Pivot of History]. *Geopolítica(s)*, vol. 1, no. 2, pp. 301–19.

Mackinlay Ferreirós, A. 2011. 'Las ambiciones marítimas de China' [China's Maritime Ambitions]. Opinion Document No. 6, Instituto Español de Estudios Estratégicos, January.

Martins, Carlos Eduardo. 2011. *Globalização, dependência e neoliberalismo na América Latina* [Globalization, Dependency and Neoliberalism in Latin America]. São Paulo: Boitempo.

Merino, Gabriel E. 2014. 'Lucha entre polos de poder por la configuración del orden mundial. El escenario actual' [Fight Between Poles of Power for the Configuration of the World Order. The Current Scenario]. *Revista de Estudios Estratégicos*, no. 1 (1st semester), pp. 13–35.

———. 2016. 'Tensiones mundiales, multipolaridad relativa y bloques de poder en una nueva fase de la crisis del orden mundial. Perspectivas de América Latina' [World Tensions, Relative Multipolarity and Power Blocs in a New Phase of the World Order Crisis. Latin American Perspectives]. *Geopolítica(s)*, vol. 2, no. 7.

———. 2017. 'Proyectos estratégicos e integración regional en América Latina. El surgimiento de la Alianza del Pacífico, el fortalecimiento del regionalismo abierto y el retroceso del regionalismo autónomo' [Strategic Projects and Regional Integration in Latin America. The Emergence of the Pacific Alliance, the Strengthening of Open Regionalism and the Decline of Autonomous Regionalism]. *Relaciones Internacionales*, vol. 26, no. 52, pp. 17–37.

———. 2018a. 'Los tratados comerciales y las luchas globales en la era Trump' [Trade Treaties and Global Struggles in the Trump Era]. *Realidad Económica*, no. 313, pp. 9–40.

———. 2018b. 'Trump: la fractura en Estados Unidos y sus implicancias en la transición histórica actual' [Trump: The Fracture in the United States and Its Implications in the Current Historical Transition]. In *Estados Unidos contra el mundo: Trump y la nueva geopolítica* [United States Against the World: Trump and the New Geopolitics], edited by Casandra Castorena Sánchez, Marco A. Gandásegui, Leandro Ariel Morgenfeld. Buenos Aires: CLACSO.

———. 2019. 'Guerra Comercial y América Latina' [Trade War and Latin America]. *Revista de Relaciones Internacionales de la UNAM*, no. 134, pp. 67–98.

———, and Nicolás Trivi. 2019. 'La Nueva Ruta de la Seda y la disputa por el poder mundial' [The New Silk Road and The Dispute for World Power]. In *China: una nueva estrategia geopolítica y global. La iniciativa de la Franja y la Ruta* [China: A New Geopolitical and Global Strategy. The Belt and Road Initiative], edited by L. Bogado, M. Caubet and F. Staiano. La Plata: Instituto de Relaciones Internacionales and Centro de Estudios Chinos de la UNLP.

Ning, Su, and Yang Chuankai. 2018. '"Silk Road Cities': Characteristics and development significance of urban pivots along the "Belt and Road"'. *The Belt & Road Studies*, vol. 2, Autumn.

Parra Pérez, Águeda. 2017. 'OBOR: las 5 claves de la mayor iniciativa de infraestructuras mundial liderada por China' [OBOR: The 5 Keys to the World's Largest Infrastructure Initiative Led by China], Opinion Document No. 113, Instituto Español de Estudios Estratégicos, November 14.

Stavridis, James. 2014. 'Vladimir Putin hates the TTIP'. *Foreign Policy*, November 19.

Summers, Larry. 2014. 'Reflections on the "New Secular Stagnation Hypothesis"'. In *Secular Stagnation: Facts, Causes and Cures*, edited by Coen Teulings and Richard Baldwin. London: CEPR.

Wallerstein, Immanuel. 2006. *La decadencia del poder estadounidense* [The Decline of Power of the United States]. Buenos Aires: Le Monde Diplomatique, Capital Intelectual.

Zhu, X. 2012. 'Understanding China's Growth: Past, Present, and Future'. *Journal of Economic Perspectives*, vol. 26, no. 4, pp. 103–24.

CONTRIBUTORS

EMILIANO LÓPEZ is an economist and Assistant Professor at the University of La Plata. He also works as a researcher for National Scientific and Technical Research Council (CONICET, Buenos Aires, Argentina) and Tricontinental: Institute for Social Research, Buenos Aires Office.

UTSA PATNAIK and PRABHAT PATNAIK are Professors Emerita and Emeritus respectively at the Centre for Economic Studies and Planning, School of Social Sciences at Jawaharlal Nehru University. They are among the leading Marxist political economists in the world and have authored numerous books and contributed articles to a range of journals in the course of their long academic careers.

JOHN SMITH is an independent researcher and writer based in Sheffield, United Kingdom. He did his PhD from the University of Sheffield. He is the author of *Imperialism in the Twenty-First Century: Globalization, Super-Exploitation, and Capitalism's Final Crisis* (2016), which received the first Paul A. Baran–Paul M. Sweezy Memorial Award by the Monthly Review Foundation for an original monograph on the political economy of imperialism.

E. AHMET TONAK is a political economist who teaches at the Economics Department, University of Massachusetts Amherst. He is the author and editor of several books including *Measuring the Wealth of Nations: The Political Economy of National Accounts* (with Anwar Shaikh), *Turkey in Transition: New Perspectives* (edited with Irvin Schick) and *Marxism and Classes* (edited with Sungur Savran and Kurtar Tanyılmaz). He is also a member of Tricontinental: Institute for Social Research.

ATILIO A. BORÓN is a political scientist and sociologist. He has been a professor at the Social Sciences Faculty of the University of

Buenos Aires since 1986. He is a senior researcher at CONICET. He is the author of many books including *State, Capitalism, and Democracy in Latin America* (1991), *Empire and Imperialism: A Critical Reading of Michael Hardt and Antonio Negri* (2002), *Twenty-first Century Socialism: Is There Life After Neoliberalism?* (2008), and most recently, *América Latina en la Geopolítica del Imperialismo* (2012).

GABRIEL E. MERINO is a sociologist who specializes in the social analysis of politics and economy in contemporary Argentina. He is a professor at the National University of La Plata and a researcher at CONICET.